C000178145

THE
DOUBTED

An FBI Psychics Novel

Shiloh Walker

THE DOUBTED
Copyright © 2018 Shiloh Walker, Inc.
Cover Design © Angela Waters

For information contact :
Shiloh Walker
PO Box 976
Jeffersonville IN 47131
www.shilohwalker.com

ISBN 9781495639241

First Edition: May 2018

DEDICATION

For everybody who keeps asking if there would be more FBI stories...this one is for you.

A SPECIAL THANK YOU

This story was made possible with the help of patrons.

Samantha-Anne
Karp Hauser
Tricia M.
EvilE
Michaela
Sarah M.
Carla
Cecilia R.
Natalie H.
Larry Omans
Serena M.
Tantris Hernandez
Nicole Amentas
A.J.Morrison
Holly C.
Nikki
Maggie Walker

Michelle B.
Heather
Elizabeth R
S. Kayne
Debbie L.
Sarah B
Diana S.
Roger S.
Noelle A.
Teresa R.
Monica
Julie Stranburg
Suzanne C.
Tammy A.
Clare
Farah

CHAPTER ONE

"It's just a headache."

When her friend tried to shine a light in her eyes, Nyrene Goldman averted her head. It was probably more than a headache and she'd go to a walk-in clinic when she got off work, but if that cranky, irritable codger they worked for came by the triage room and saw them, they'd never hear the end of it.

"You were in a wreck," Michelle said, her eyes narrowed. Her hair, currently dyed a shade that couldn't decide if it was a deep red or purple, was pulled back into a ponytail. Small tendrils had escaped. She couldn't tame the frizzy curls for the life of her. They bounced around her face as she shook her head. "You didn't go to the hospital. You know better than that. For fuck's sake, Nye, you're a nurse."

"Which explains everything," Nye said, grinning despite the pounding in her head. "I'm a nurse...ergo, that means I'm a lousy patient. And it wasn't a bad wreck, okay? Somebody just ran up into my bumper. If I hadn't been pissed off at that son of a bitch, Paxton, it wouldn't have happened."

"Well, hey, I'm all for blaming him for everything." Michelle grinned. "But I'm not sure how you can blame him for this."

"Easy. I wasn't paying attention when I slowed at the stop sign. If I had been, I would have seen that idiot kid joyriding and maybe I would have moved quicker...I dunno. But I'm *fine*. I'm just supposed to work on inputting data for the new system today anyway. I'll hide in a room and take it easy, okay?"

"Staring at a screen isn't going to help that headache. And what if you have a concussion? How hard did you hit the window? Does your neck hurt?"

"Not that hard." She went to shrug and then thought better of it. "My neck is stiff. As expected. And I've got muscle relaxers. I take them anyway, remember? I'll go to a clinic tonight, okay? I just wasn't going to the ER."

She couldn't *afford* it.

Michelle looked like she wanted to argue, but a door slammed and they heard a familiar grumbling fill the hallway.

"Dr. Evil is here," Michelle said under her breath. "How long until the new guy takes over?"

"Three months." Nye moved off the bench and toward the cabinet, as if she'd been checking supplies. Each motion made the pounding in her head increase and she had the insane desire to grab some of the cotton balls and shove them into her ears to silence all the noise. "Three damn months."

"That's four months too long."

But Nyrene barely heard her. The low-level buzzing in her head seemed to drown out everything else.

* * * * *

Sweat dripped down her spine. A cold, icy sweat, but Nye tried to ignore it. She just had to get through the rest of the afternoon.

Granted, every minute seemed like torture.

She almost felt like she was having a cocktail party— inside her skull. Everything was so *noisy*. She kept hearing whispers and curses, except the words made no sense.

I'm going crazy, she thought, and she was more than a little afraid she wasn't wrong.

The chart in front of her— her gut churned. Images flashed across her vision. The girl... Nye knew her. Barely. A teen, in and out of foster care, recently reunited with her mom. There was a boyfriend. She'd come in recently...

What was her name?

Hailey...

Even as she thought of the name, she saw the girl.

In a car. Parked in front of a house. There was a flash, like lightning, illuminating the address. Inside the car, a girl struggled—*can't breathe*. As if she'd said the words,

Nyrene heard them. And Hailey struggled as a boy wrapped his hands around her throat—

"What the *fuck*?" Nyrene said, shoving back from the desk and standing up. Her legs wobbled and she slammed into the wall as they tried to give out from under her.

She rubbed her throat, that odd sensation of not being able to breathe gone.

Maybe she had a brain bleed. She'd hit her head so hard, blood was leaking inside her skull and she was going crazy. That could make her see things that weren't there, hear things that weren't there, couldn't it?

This wasn't the first thing like this she'd imagined today.

She'd had to beg a ride from a friend and as they pulled away from the curb, her friend Jazzy had told her, *You look like shit.*

Except Jazzy hadn't said anything.

Nyrene had heard the *words*, but Jazzy's mouth hadn't moved, not even once.

It was past noon. She'd planned on trying to work straight through, get her eight in so she could leave, but maybe that wasn't such a good idea.

"I need food." The thought of that made the nausea even worse, but yeah, she needed to eat. Get a drink, stop making herself go blind from inputting Dr. Evil's paper records into the new electronic charting system the new doctor would use.

It should have been done years ago, but Evil refused.

Dr. Evil—Dr. Evered, in reality—was sixty-nine years old and the meanest son of a bitch she'd ever worked for. She knew she needed to be at home, but Evil didn't believe in sick days—not for his employees. Still, he couldn't deny her a lunch so she made her way down the hall to the break room. It wasn't much bigger than one of the patient exam rooms and the other three full-time employees were in there, gathered around a small table.

Michelle looked at her and swore. "You look like you're going to pass out, Nye."

She gave Michelle a game smile. "Oh, I'm fine. It's those damn files. How long until we're free of Evil again?"

It was a familiar game, and they all knew, to the day, when he was leaving. Although, really, just then, Nye couldn't remember. And Michelle wasn't answering.

"I'm serious, Nye. You look bad."

"I just need some food." She stared dumbly at the table, realized she hadn't brought anything.

"You sit." Heather patted her shoulder.

Then, clear as day, Nyrene heard the words, *Maybe some food will help.*

Nyrene fought the urge to flinch under that touch. Staring at Heather, she offered a weak smile. "Yeah. Yeah that will help."

"I made soup last night. I'll get you some of the leftovers. I always bring too much. Maybe some food will help."

Nyrene had to bite back her hysterical laughter, the urge to say, *You just said that!*

Because Heather *hadn't* said anything about food helping...at least not twice.

Again, Nyrene was hearing the words, but Heather hadn't actually *said* it aloud the first time.

"Soup sounds good," she said wanly. Maybe it would help. But even as she thought of it, her mind went fuzzy and vague, spinning back to the girl who kept sneaking into her head. Hailey. Her name was Hailey. Curled up on her side, crying.

"Hailey...Hailey...Hailey..."

"Who's Hailey?"

Nye jerked her head up as Heather put the soup in front of her. "What?"

"You said Hailey."

Michelle, Heather and Judith eyed her oddly. She would have shrugged, but it would have sent pain shrieking through her head, and if she had more pain, she thought she'd cry.

"I'm just remembering something from one of the records I was inputting." She couldn't even smile without it hurting. Looking down at the soup, she breathed in. "It smells good."

No.

No, it didn't.

But Heather gave her a spoon and she was able to close her hand around it and take a couple of bites. It was actually rather soothing, gliding down to her belly. Felt good.

But her gut started to rebel at the next bite and she put

down the spoon.

"Nye, you need to eat."

"I can't." She swallowed and focused on the bowl, the table. On the sound of Michelle's voice—on *anything* but the fact that she kept hearing *other* voices. "I think... I think I need to go see that doctor."

"Yes. You *should*." The relief in Michelle's voice was palpable. "But...shit, can you drive?"

Drive? She didn't even have a car *to* drive. Not right now. She'd had Jazzy drive her to work, but how was she supposed to...

Her mind slid sideways, the thought drifting away on a wave of pain. Images shifted, reformed. The girl.

No. Don't think about...

Voices churned in her ears. Dully, Nye stared at the little TV she'd brought to the office earlier in the year. They had to keep the volume almost nonexistent and honestly, they had it in there more to thumb their noses at Evil than anything else. It wasn't the noise that caught her attention, though.

It was something to look at, to focus on, to think about—

And then she saw the words.

Those bright red words. Staring at them made it feel like her eyes were vibrating in their sockets.

Corruption Suspected in Leighton's Police Department.

"Police," she said, her lips numb.

Suddenly, the images of Hailey disappeared, replaced by something else.

Screams. Blood. Gunshots.

A pair of ice-blue eyes, frozen in a mask of death.

Familiar eyes.

She shuddered as those eyes began to fill with life, presence.

"Nyrene. That's a pretty name."

Those ice-blue eyes thawed as he studied her. Nyrene felt stupid. She'd fallen apart on him, all but soaking the sturdy dark material of his uniform.

"You okay there, Nyrene?"

She sucked in a breath. "I'm fine."

No, she wasn't. But she would be. As soon as she forgot about that son of a bitch she'd wasted three years on.

Paxton Wallace—accountant, father of two, the one she'd thought for sure was the ideal man.

Only he'd lied. The bastard had lied. He wasn't an accountant. He had two kids...in this state. And one across the river in Mississippi. Another three in Tennessee.

He wasn't an accountant. He was a con artist. And the money he'd talked her into giving him—some of her hard-earned savings. He'd claimed he could triple the money.

"I'm so stupid!"

There was a soft sigh. A hand stroked her shoulder one more time. "It doesn't look like you were at fault, Ms. Goldman." He had a soft, soothing voice. Smooth and rich, like dark, decadent coffee laced with the finest whiskey.

She stiffened, pulled away, every muscle in her body screaming.

"Officer..."

"Deverall," he said. "Officer Deverall."

Her mind shifted. Roiled. Those ice-blue eyes, wide and locked. A neat, bloody hole between them, a gun in his hand—

And then bloody red...again.

Local officer, celebrated war hero Bennett Deverall was gunned—

Voices shrieked in her head, blurring together.

Officer Ben Deverall was suspected of corruption. During the operation to bring him in, he resisted arrest—

"No, no, no, no!"

Darkness swam in and grabbed her. Pulled her under.

Nye didn't even mind. Because for once the pain in her head was gone and there was nothing but sweet, sweet silence.

CHAPTER TWO

"Deverall! Hey, hey...Ben!"

He ignored it.

The last person he wanted to talk to right now was a reporter. Not even Meredith Russell. Maybe especially not Meredith Russell. Maybe she was a decent reporter, and maybe she was a decent human being, as far as reporters went.

But he knew exactly what was going on in the department right now. He'd known what was going on for quite a while, actually. He'd been bypassed for promotions, but that was okay—he didn't want to advance in a department like this one.

He'd waited, bided his time, collected his evidence, until he knew who he could trust.

Then IAB came to him.

He'd almost breathed a sigh of relief, although talking to the rat squad still left a bad taste in his mouth. Dirty cops, though, were no cops at all.

But somebody in the damn rat squad was a rat. He'd had a bad feeling about it for a couple of weeks, so he'd done his *own* investigation—leaking out information just to see what happened.

And fuck if he wasn't right.

Now he had a target on his back. Anything he did or said now was only going to make it worse.

Meredith wasn't the type to give up easily. As he headed down the hallway to speak to his witness, he could hear her high heels clacking on the floor behind him. He closed his eyes for a brief moment. *A break*, he thought. *Just a bit of one, please.*

He accepted the fact that he was never going to get out of uniform, not in this town. He had accepted the fact that he might not even survive the fallout once all was said and done and he passed on what he knew.

But he'd at least like to finish up and tie off some loose ends. A hand closed around his arm. He came to a stop and glared down at Meredith. "I'm working," he said, slowly and clearly. "I've got a witness to talk to. I've got reports to file, a job to do."

"Come on, Ben. Five minutes. You can give me five minutes. Off the record." She gave him a charming smile, one that showed the dimple in her cheek. She leaned in as she spoke, offering him a view of something equally as charming as her dimple and her smile.

But it had been that smile, that dimple, among other things, that had landed him in this mess. Then he stopped and mentally adjusted his line of thinking. That wasn't fair. It wasn't her fault that three-fourths of the cops in this town were corrupt.

"Look, just a few questions..." She smiled at him—wide, winsome and pretty. "I'll hold the answers until you say otherwise."

He knew better. One of the things he'd leaked had been to her. She'd promised to hold *those* answers, too. He'd known she'd leak them, but it also proved one thing for certain.

He couldn't trust her.

"Here's a comment for you..." He leaned in, paused until she'd all but stopped breathing as she waited. "No comment. I'm done. Now please let me get my job done."

He stepped around her and headed on down the hall.

"Come on. You know this isn't over. You know it goes deeper. Give me more. Between us." Now her voice sounded rougher, harsher. He stopped and looked back at her, and in her eyes he could see the frustration he'd been feeling the past few months. No, for him, it had been longer. What he didn't see was the one thing he needed to see—fear.

Once more, he went back to her and held her gaze. "Yeah. I know it isn't over. Maybe you'll try to say it's between us. But it won't be just between us. Everybody knows who talks to you. And the target that has been on my back for the past few months just now went from red and white to neon green and white. Every single one of them are going to come gunning for me now. I was trying to get things settled up before that happened. Now there's no time. Let me do my job while I still can."

"Five minutes," she said, her voice going flat. "I've got information for *you*, too."

He went stiff and turned to look at her. "Don't bullshit me, Meredith."

"I'm not." She cocked her head to the side. "Quid pro quo, Officer. You can decide to pass it on...or not. But it's good info."

He swore and tipped his head back, staring up at the ceiling. Then he nodded tersely. "I have to talk to somebody first. You can meet me outside. Probably in twenty minutes."

She gave him a smile. "Excellent."

She strode past him, heading down the hall.

*   *   *   *   *

I shouldn't have eaten that chicken.

Please...please...please don't let my mama be having a heart attack.

Why the fuck all these people gotta be here? I need to get this done and get back to work...

I hate the smell of hospitals.

That man had better be out there...

The voices were a roar in her head and Nyrene couldn't block them out. Staring hard at the floor, she tried to focus on *nothing* but the little flecks of blue in the tile and the sound of her own breathing.

Click click click—a pair of murder-red heels cut across her field of vision. As though her gaze had been forcibly drawn up, she found herself staring at the blonde woman now walking away from her.

The blonde was beautiful, her coat red as blood, her hair falling in a smooth, straight curtain all the way down her back. She paused near the door and glanced back and Nyrene saw her face.

It's News Reporter Barbie, some hysterical part of her brain said, a mad little giggle underscoring the words. *Coming to you live from the edge of madness.*

The woman glanced at Nyrene and Nyrene almost gagged on the bile that rushed up her throat as she gasped and nausea swamped her.

She knew her—

Please, please, I don't want to die!

The voice screamed inside Nyrene's head and she clapped her hands over her ears as images washed over her. The woman striding toward her car. Heels clicking on the ground. Somebody calls her name. She turns, looks, rolls her eyes. Irritated, so irritated. *I'm busy. I've got a meet with a source in a few minutes. I already told you, I'm done with this.*

A hand reaches out—touches her cheek. Skin, soft...

She smacks him, irritation bleeding into anger...then stark, cold fear.

What are you doing— No!

The scream, muffled against a hand. *Please, please, I don't want to die!*

The gunshot, also muffled—a loud *pop* instead of a booming ricochet.

Eyes wide, stunned. Then, as if in slow motion, a bullet piercing her just between the eyebrows, the hole small and neat, then bloody.

Her eyes went glassy and blank.

Dead.

Whimpering, Nyrene curled into a ball and hugged her knees to her chest as the pain and shivering spread through her, overtaking her entire body.

"Ms. Goldman?"

The sound of her name had her whimpering, sinking even deeper into the unforgiving seat as the pain sliced and cut through her. She felt like her brain was being fed through a meat grinder, and all the while a reel of the images she'd just seen played through her mind over and over and over.

She started to rock, moaning under her breath. *No, no, no, nonononono...*

A hand touched her arm.

Another flash echoed through her mind and she struck out and blinding pain flooded her.

Somebody shouted.

Another hand grabbed her.

Then another, as voices rose all around her.

Dev heard the commotion.

He closed his eyes, let his head fall back. The last thing he wanted to do was respond to the shouting and the voices he heard coming from around the corner.

Just go. Just walk away.

A hospital security guard ran by him.

He could walk away, right?

But the badge he carried, the reason *he* had decided to carry that fucking badge, wouldn't let him walk away, so instead of heading out that door to meet up with Meredith, he headed out to see what all the shouting was about.

It involved a woman, struggling on the floor in the waiting room.

Two—no, make that three—of the hospital staff held her down.

She was sweating and panicked. Her olive skin had an odd tinge to it, her raven hair fell into her face. Familiarity pricked at him. It hit him then—the wreck. Last night.

Somebody grabbed her quivering leg and she tensed, whimpered again.

He moved to help and her head swung. "*No, no, no, no...*"

Kneeling, he touched her arm. She immediately stiffened, then turned her head blindly toward him.

"What's wrong with her?"

"Fucking crazy," somebody muttered from nearby. It wasn't one of the medical personnel, but the doctor across from him had a look in his eyes as he met Dev's gaze. *Yeah, that about sums it up.*

He frowned. "I know this woman. She was in a car wreck last night. She's not—"

She arched, thrashed. Somebody came rushing up with a cart. He recognized the look of it, even if he'd forgotten the name. Instinct kicked in and Dev reached up and caught the doctor's arm even as he reached out.

"She's not crazy," he said softly. "She was in a wreck and hit her head on the window, pretty hard from what I could see. I tried to get her to come in, but she wouldn't. You sure you should go pumping her full of something if you're not sure what you're treating?"

"I know a hallucination when I see one," the doctor snapped.

"A hallucination?" Dev looked down. What *he* saw was a terrified woman, and the more people struggled to hold

14

her down, the more terrified she became. "I see a scared woman. Why don't you try having them let go for ten damn seconds?"

"That *scared* woman hauled off and kicked me," a nurse said, struggling to hold down the woman's legs.

"For no reason?" Dev demanded, his hands still on the woman's arm. She was tense, whimpering, but not trying to fight. Just...trembling. Terrified.

"The woman scared her."

The voice came from the side. An old man sat in a wheelchair, an oxygen mask in his hand, a disapproving look in his eyes as he stared at everybody. "Poor girl been sittin' there," he said, his voice thick with an accent that made his words almost indistinguishable. "Over two hours, she been sittin' there. Cryin' like a broken doll and shakin', shiverin'. I don' think she even know where she is."

He nodded at the nurse. "That one, she come out, call her name. The girl don' even hear her."

The nurse opened her mouth. "Sir, this doesn't concern you."

"Ain't none of us *concern* you," he sneered. "I sit here for over an hour, can't hardly breathe and nobody come check on me. That girl, cryin' and shakin' and holdin' her head like it done split apart. Then you scare the shit out of her, grabbin' her like that and you wonder why she kick you? Somebody grab and shake me like that, I kick 'em, too."

As the nurse went red, Dev looked at the doctor. "It sounds to me like she reacted, not like she attacked."

Slowly, he nodded and then looked at his staff. "Everybody, let go."

The next sixty seconds were tense. But all she did was lie there, trembling.

She didn't open her eyes, didn't move. She just lay there.

When the doctor spoke, she flinched, as though even the sound of his voice hurt.

"Ma'am?"

Under the warm gold of her skin, she paled and Dev felt his heart twist. Why hadn't he insisted she go to the hospital? How much damage had that hit to her head done?

"Do you remember her name?"

"Yeah. Nyrene. Nyrene Goldman."

The doctor looked at him. "Good memory, Officer Deverall."

Not so much. I just remember because some sick part of me was wishing I hadn't met her because I was working a scene, that I wasn't in the middle of the biggest mess of my life.

Then there was the dream he'd had last night.

She'd starred, front and center, with that porn-star mouth and her wide, dark eyes.

It was the only dream he could recall having in months that hadn't ended with blood and screams...or him staring down the barrel of a gun.

Nudging the memories out of his head, he remained where he was, keeping his hands away from her as the doctor reached out. Although her eyes were shut, she immediately twisted away as though she'd sensed his intention. The doctor stilled. "Ms. Goldman, do you know where you are?"

Her lids came up.

Dev found himself caught in the gold of her eyes. Wide-set, that impossible shade of gold, and right now, cloudy and fogged by pain. Fear.

"Ms. Goldman?"

"Hospital," she said softly. "At hospital."

"Good. Good..." The doctor nodded and then gave Dev a look. "I need some room. We need to—"

She shot out a hand, caught Dev's arm. "Help me," she said, her voice suddenly clear, urgency underlying it.

Caught off guard, he stared at her. "You're at the hospital, Nye— Ms. Goldman. The doctors will help you. We should get you up, back to a room."

She opened her mouth, looked around. Then snapped it closed. "You." She swallowed, as though it hurt to do so. "Help... Can you help me up?"

Nyrene was almost certain she'd lost her mind.

That part—the part that was still capable of rational thought, the part that had been appalled at the way she'd kicked and screamed and bucked when people were touching her, just trying to help—was sitting back, quietly shaking her head. That part of her mind was like a

16

passenger in her head—just along for the ride now. She'd gone from shrieking *Are you crazy, calm your ass down* to just...sitting there while her mind processed everything.

Dissociative break.

The nurse inside her coolly processed it. You're having a dissociative break. You're going crazy, but it's okay, Nye. There's help for this.

The cop with the ice-blue eyes continued to watch her and she stared at him as though he was the only person in the room. For her, he might as well have been.

She had to keep him with her.

Had to.

Even as that calm, cool voice in her head assured her that everything was fine, despite her break with reality, it also insisted that keeping this sexy cop, with his pretty blue eyes, with her was of utmost importance.

Every time she closed her eyes, she understood why, too.

The woman hadn't been found yet.

She was already dead.

Nye didn't understand how she knew that.

But when he'd appeared in her line of sight, those awful, unreal images had begun to spin through her mind. This man, moving out of the garage, an impatient look on his face. He caught sight of the woman and started to rush to her side...and then he was surrounded by cops.

Four of them, two who wore the same uniform he did, two in suits.

Drop your weapon, Deverall. Don't make us do this. He'd smiled as he said it.

Dev had just stared at him, a grim look of acceptance on his face.

Then he'd turned around and just stood there. *If you're going to do this—*

The noise in her head faded and even the pain ebbed briefly.

Now there was only nausea.

And fear.

She *wanted* to believe she was crazy, but she had a bad, bad feeling. No. It went deeper than that. She had a gut-deep assurance that there was a dead woman in the garage, and men with guns waiting...for *this* man.

"Nyrene?"

She jumped at the sound of his voice and looked up at him.

He gave her a gentle smile. "I'm going to let the doctors take over now, okay? They need to—"

"No!"

She laced her fingers with his, gripped tightly, so tightly her hand hurt, but she wouldn't let go. "You can't leave! Don't leave me!"

"Where is he?"

The low voice came from the shadows, raspy from years of cigarettes, years of alcohol. Although he was all but shaking with fear, he didn't let that show in his voice. This was all under control.

Even if the dumbfuck in front of him had jumped the gun.

"He'll be here." Said dumbfuck gave him an irritated look. "Why are you so worked up? The cameras are out. She parked about as far out of the way as she can be and still be in the damn garage and nobody can see here, where she is. He'll be here. He just sent her a text saying he was on his way. If he says he's on his way, he's on his way. Fucker is practically a Boy Scout."

"The times aren't going to match if he isn't here soon."

Idly, he entertained the idea of shoving his gun into the idiot's side, pulling the trigger, saving himself, his boss, and taxpayers a lot of grief. In the long run, this man was going to be trouble. He'd already been investigated twice— idiot criminals, complaining that they'd been mistreated. His partner, though, he liked to use force, and a lot of it. He'd cross the line at some point. If he just ended it now...

Another minute ticked by.

Another minute.

As the five-minute mark approached, he realized he was starting to sweat.

If they couldn't get Deverall *here*, on the scene with Russell, they had problems.

His phone buzzed.

Not his official one, but the cheap, untraceable piece of shit he carried for business he didn't want traced back to him. He pulled it from his pocket. A headache began to pulse and once more, the idea of just eliminating the problem some people called his partner started to appeal to him all over again.

He flashed the display. "We have a problem."

The message was short and simple. But it spelled out what was going to add up to a lot of shit heading their way, all because his partner hadn't been able to wait.

He was still inside—some sort of problem with a patient.

CHAPTER THREE

"You're not helping."

Dr. Lovett gave him an aggravated look before shooting a glance back over his shoulder at the woman who huddled on the bed. "I don't know if she's latched on to you because of the car wreck or if there's some other reason, but this...this isn't normal and you can't keep staying at her side just because you..." He paused, floundering for words.

Dev wasn't exactly sure why he'd spent the past thirty minutes with a woman who was more than likely troubled. It didn't make sense. She'd been *fine* when he'd pulled up to handle the MVA—taking care of the report from the wreck, even trying to get her to come in to the hospital. She'd been clear and calm. Pissed, hurting, but clearly fine.

Today...

He gave a reluctant nod and looked back at her. "Just let me—"

"You should leave."

"She doesn't have any family. Nobody at all she can call." Dev knew what that was like. "Maybe *that's* why she *latched* on, as you call it. Having a familiar face when you're hurting or scared is sometimes the only thing that can pull you through. No, I can't stay, but I'm not just disappearing without telling her I'm leaving, either."

Lovett gave him a grim look, then shook his head before stepping aside.

Dev ducked back into the room. Most of the exam rooms in the emergency department were more like curtained-off partitions as they went through the expansion and remodeling, but Nyrene had been put in a private room. He had a feeling the doctors hadn't wanted her upsetting the others.

She looked up at the sound of his shoes on the linoleum and to his surprise, she gave him a tired smile. "I'm sorry."

"Ah..."

A sigh seemed to shudder out of her and she rested her head on her knees. "It's gone. That headache."

He frowned. "They're going to help you, Nye— Ms. Goldman."

As much pain as she was in, whatever was wrong, it couldn't be gone in the short time since he'd stepped outside into the hall with the doctor who'd come to evaluate her.

Her lashes lifted and he found himself looking into tired, but clear, eyes.

"I'm okay now, Officer Deverall." She slid off the exam table and he went to stop her, but she lifted her hands. "Please...um. Please don't touch me. I...I don't think I like people touching me."

He shot a look at her. *I don't think I like people touching me.*

That didn't really fit with the hugger he'd encountered last night. And she *had* been a hugger. Just one of those naturally affectionate people. It had driven him a little crazy because that soft, sweetly curved body pressed against his had done a number on him as she tried not to cry after the accident. Holding it together professionally had been easy enough—telling himself to get a grip and push it away, put it aside? Not so much.

He'd dealt with crying women before on the job. Most cops had. Some were irritating, some made him uncomfortable. Dev just took it as part of the job until last night.

He'd enjoyed every second her body had been close to his and then he'd regretted every second his body had been in uniform because there was no way he could make anything come of it, especially not now.

And not just because there was clearly something...odd going on.

She went to open the door and he blocked her. "Ms. Goldman, you need to sit down, let the doctor examine you."

"No." She smiled and it was a smile of relief, as if the

weight of the world had fallen away. "I think I just had to keep you from going into the garage."

He gaped at her, caught off guard by that statement long enough that she was able to slide past him and open the door.

The doctor was the next one to try to stop her while Dev just stood there, trying to figure out what she'd meant.

The sound of doors banging open had him looking up. It was an almost instinctive gesture.

Immediately, he backed out of the hallway as a crash team came rushing through, doctors shouting orders, nurses calling out numbers.

Distantly, he noticed that Nyrene Goldman had gone still and was staring at the team as they all but ran by.

Out of the chaos, it was almost bizarre the way his ears caught one simple phrase.

"Damn. Meredith Russell...she always wanted to get the top story...but not like this..."

His radio crackled. Instinctively, he went to respond, but instead, he found himself following the crash team. He had misunderstood. That was all.

Except he hadn't.

He was still processing that hours later after he finished giving his statement to the investigating officers— one that was very, very self-edited.

He couldn't exactly stand there and tell one of the cops he knew was dirty that he had been meeting with the reporter because she claimed she had information to pass to him about the corruption going on inside the department, now could he?

No. That wouldn't have gone over well.

He slumped in the seat of his cruiser, staring at the rain-splattered windshield, but he didn't see the rain or the blue-on-white sign of the hospital or even the flashing lights of the arriving ambulance.

He kept seeing the images the investigating officer had shown.

Meredith Russell, lying on her back, a neat entry wound in her forehead. The blood had stained her pretty blonde hair red and her wide blue eyes were glassy in death, blank.

But he could see the accusation in them.

He should have been there.

Why hadn't he—

Abruptly, he slammed a fist into the dashboard.

"Son of a bitch!"

He jammed the key into the ignition and gave it a vicious wrench, threw the car into drive and pulled out of the parking slot with a squeal of rubber on cement.

I think I just had to keep you from going into the garage.

Nyrene sat cross-legged on her couch with her laptop on her legs. The vicious pain in her head was gone, but there was an odd, muffled feeling back there. It reminded her of the way she'd felt after the orthodontist had pulled a molar and then packed it up with cotton. She kind of hoped there wouldn't be some huge stabbing pain developing as the metaphorical Novocain wore off.

Of course, it was entirely possible that she'd be back in the hospital—on the psych floor—by the time it happened.

She really was going crazy.

She'd spent a ridiculous amount on a cab ride home, and it had been a *quiet* ride—none of that noise in her head, no images, no screams.

No visions of blood or violence.

Once she'd locked herself in her home, she'd gone online. She hadn't bothered with the local news. Even if her gut was right, the news wouldn't be posted yet. The media was always hours behind what a person could find out via social sites, it seemed.

Sure enough, there on the Twitter stream for a local blogger who followed the police radio, she'd seen it.

Just in: fatality at CCH. Victim unverified, but heard the name Meredith Russell. ??? Reporter at WCLA?

A flurry of retweets and questions had followed, but the user hadn't responded or posted anything more until he had more information, and that had made Nyrene's stomach hurt.

Fuck, guys. It was MR. I caught a few things on the

radio before they switched frequencies.

That had been hours ago and she hadn't bothered to look for anything else.

Either she was going crazy and she'd hallucinated the past few hours or something else was going on.

Nyrene almost preferred to think she was going crazy. It seemed safer.

But in the back of her mind, that calm, rational voice that had tried to take over in the hospital had started to speak. This time, that voice had drowned out everything else.

This is really happening. You didn't hallucinate any of it.

That means you need to look at the other things.

Which explained how she'd found herself at this website—The Psychic Portal.

It had seemed gibberish, but finally, she'd found a contact button and although it seemed like a shot in the dark, she'd sent off an email, asking for more information.

She'd get a response in two months, when she'd either committed herself to Southern State, the only psychiatric facility available on her lousy insurance, or when all of this turned out to be a very bad dream.

She hadn't even had a chance to find another decent source when a response came back. It was a short, almost form-like, and it sent her to a questionnaire.

Ten minutes later, her head pounding, she finished it and slumped down on the couch, wanting a drink. It seemed like a dumb thing to do, considering she didn't know what was going on inside her head. She still wasn't completely ruling out some sort of traumatic brain injury, although the likelihood didn't seem high.

There was another response in her email and this was a personal response.

Hello
I apologize for what seems like tedious and needless steps before we allow anybody to join us here at the Portal, but I'm sure you can understand...we get a lot of flakes, fakes and fools here.
You, however, are a different sort of beast and we'd love to

have you.

There are actually two portals here. A public face, the one we give to the flakes, fakes and fools, and the one real portal. Below is the link you'll need to set up your account at the real portal.

Please pick a username that will help you remain anonymous and never share any personal details. As you can imagine, the world isn't a safe place, but there are many who would prey on the gifted, and while you struggle to understand what is happening to you, you will be more vulnerable than you can imagine.

Welcome...and I hope you can find some information to help with your headaches. I've been there. They are horrid. Let me know if I can help.

Phantom

The entire message left her squirming uncomfortably.

But the final paragraph had her slowly setting the laptop down, as though she had suddenly found herself holding something quite deadly.

Swallowing, she stood and backed away one step, then another.

She hadn't said anything about her headaches.

Not a damn thing.

A hard fist slammed on the door and she jumped, unable to muffle the shriek before it escaped her.

Find out what's going on.

A rough, masculine voice.

A familiar one.

Her head started to pound as she looked away from the computer to stare at her door.

There was another knock and she eased her way around the coffee table, leaving the laptop where it was, as it was.

She'd think about that email, and all its assorted creepiness, later. After she saw who was at the door.

You know. Her imagination filled in the blanks—big and blond, with his ice-blue eyes and impassive features, Ben Deverall was a mouthwatering piece of work. Too bad the terror had dried all the spit from her mouth.

"Ms. Goldman, please open the door," a brusque voice said. "It's Officer Bennett Deverall with the Clary Police Department."

The sound of his voice didn't do anything to soothe her uneasiness.

Why couldn't she have been wrong?

Why couldn't he be the Easter Bunny? A cute little girl selling Girl Scout cookies? *Anybody* other than the cop, because that would mean she *hadn't* just *known*.

She swiped her hands on the soft cotton of her pajama pants and paused for a second to look down at herself. She'd changed when she got home, into something warm and comfortable and soft, desperate for the comfort. Now, though, she wished she hadn't.

The long-sleeved cotton shirt wasn't quite thick enough to disguise the fact that she wasn't wearing a bra and the slogan written across it in vivid, pink font was funny, if you knew the context. She'd gotten it at a book convention she'd attended a few years ago.

But Dev wouldn't know the context and now she had to open the door with some rather risqué words scrawled across her boobs like an invitation—*You've been a bad boy...go to my room.*

The irony of it all—if it wasn't a terrible situation she found herself in, having Bennett Deverall in her room wouldn't bother her a bit.

Groaning at how pathetic she was, she reached for the door, keeping the security chain in place as she peeked out.

He stood with his hands on his hips, head slumped, but at the sound of the door he slowly lifted his head. Rain drenched him, clinging to golden-blonde hair, high cheekbones, and rolling down a jaw so hard it could have been carved from granite.

"Hello," she said and the unsteady sound of her voice made her want to pound her head against the door.

"I'd like to speak with you." The rain started to come down even harder and the pitiful excuse she had for a porch didn't offer much protection at all. "If I could...?"

She undid the chain and opened the door, stepping back. Manners had been drilled into her. If it hadn't been raining, maybe she could have kept him outside for a few minutes, but not in that downpour.

He came in, rain falling around him to puddle on the

floor.

His gaze swept over her and lingered on the shirt.

"Let me get you a towel." She spun around.

"That's not necessary."

"Neither is it necessary for you to drip water all over my floor," she responded, painfully aware of the fact that he was following her down the narrow hall to her bathroom.

She imagined it was a safety thing, a cop thing, and she tried not to think about how closely he followed her, or anything else.

It was funny, trying to blank her mind, though, because when she tried to *stop* thinking about him, she found herself thinking about all the little things she hadn't even realized she knew. Like, she hadn't been aware of how hard his muscles had felt under her hands when he'd helped her stand earlier, or how wide his shoulders were.

But she was remembering it all in acute detail now.

Grabbing a towel from the rod, she turned around and thrust it at him. "Here," she said, her voice tight, rusty.

He took it with a sigh and nodded. "Thank you." He stepped back and gestured.

She slid out of the bathroom, conscious of him rubbing the towel over his face, across his almost ruthlessly short hair. When she led him into her small living room, she caught sight of him in the reflective glass of the windows and saw him drag the towel down his neck, head tipped back.

Nyrene curled her hands into fists as she turned around.

"What can I help you with?"

A rush of heat swamped her as an image assailed her. *Take off that damn shirt...*

His voice echoed in her mind and subconsciously, she wrapped her arms around her middle, hiding the way her nipples had tightened and were now stabbing into the material of her shirt.

Take off that damn shirt...

Self-preservation made her desperate and she had the insane desire to just slam a door, build a wall, shut a window—*anything* to keep her from hearing everything that seemed to flood her head now, the images that crowded into her mind...like his hands grabbing the hem of her shirt, peeling it upward.

She spun away and stared at the window. *Close the damn window!*

The images in her head cut off and the heated rush that had swamped her disappeared. In the breadth of a second.

Thank God.

Take off that damn shirt for starters, Dev thought sourly. Then his mind underwent a short circuit as he thought of her doing just that, peeling the black cotton away, revealing golden skin and a body that he was already too aware of.

She wasn't wearing a bra, a fact he hadn't been able to ignore when she opened the door, and now he also knew that her full breasts had tight, prominent nipples and he wanted to see how she'd react when he rolled them between his fingers, then toyed with them, using his tongue and teeth.

Not what you're here for. Get your brain out of your dick. He lowered the towel and looked around. "Mind if I have a seat?"

"Feel free."

He went to sit on the only chair and then stopped, sighing as the water continued to drip off. He had his own little rain puddle. "Maybe I should just stand," he said, shaking his head.

"That's not—"

"It's fine." Waving toward the couch, he said, "Feel free, though. I'll try to keep this short."

He instinctively turned toward the electric fireplace she had on. It was tucked against one wall, giving off a somewhat realistic impression of an actual flame, and the heat felt good, although it served to remind him of how miserably uncomfortable his uniform was.

There was a faint chiming sound and he glanced over just as she looked at her laptop. She caught her lip between her teeth and although she tried to be subtle, he noticed the way she looked at him, then away. And the way she casually closed her laptop. Just a little too casually.

"I only have a couple of questions," he said, schooling his face into the polite, blank mask he'd perfected ages ago.

"Actually, just one."

"I don't know if there's much of anything else I can tell you about the accident," she said softly. "I already called my insurance. My agent tells me the fault is clear. It will probably take a while to get it settled, but—"

"It's not about the accident." He moved over, eyed the wide, fat table and then decided, the hell with courtesy. He was looking over the edge into his grave anyway. Sitting down, he stared at her, eye to eye, wondering if she was yet another stumbling block they'd thrown at him, or if she was just another innocent bystander. He had to know— stumbling blocks could be dealt with. He was tired of innocent bystanders paying the price, though.

"Oh?" Her eyes widened ever so slightly and he couldn't help but notice the darker striations of brown that splintered the golden color. She seemed all about golden warmth with those eyes and her skin.

Her hair, though, was black as night, straight as rain.

Deliberately, he clenched one hand into a fist.

Thinking about her hair, her eyes, her mouth, her ass—not going to help him learn what he needed to learn.

"The hospital," he said.

And those golden eyes went blank.

"I'd like to know exactly what that display at the hospital was about, Ms. Goldman. Why were you so determined to keep me out of the parking garage?"

"I..." She said nothing else, just shook her head.

"Okay, then I do have a second question." Leaning in until only a few scant inches separated them, he held her gaze for a long moment, listening as her breathing hitched, as her pupils spiked. "What does it have to do with the dead woman they found out there?"

She sucked in a breath of air and he wanted to swear. He wanted to hit something. He wanted to grab her and shake her and he wanted to scream.

Because he saw it in her eyes—she wasn't some innocent bystander.

Somehow, she was connected.

Nyrene Goldman, this woman who intoxicated him and made him want to forget everything that didn't involve soft sheets and naked flesh, was involved with the men who wanted him dead.

CHAPTER FOUR

"I don't know."

She was almost afraid to say even those words.

His eyes had somehow gone terribly cold and it terrified her, but she had to say something.

"You don't know," he said, the words condescending. "A woman is murdered only moments after you grab on to me and demand I stay with you. And you *knew* something was going on. I can see it in your eyes, but you don't know how it's connected."

"No." She winced and got up, sidling around the table, desperate to get away from eyes that had practically turned to ice. She couldn't hear anything in her head now and part of her *wanted* to, even as she feared what it might be.

A nervous breath jittered out of her and she thought of that window—the one she'd imagined slamming shut.

She's connected...

His voice slid inside her mind just like that as she imagined the window *gone*.

That low-level buzz returned, voices and murmurs and whispers that she could not begin to distinguish.

I don't believe this.

The words were his, not hers. Although he hadn't spoken.

The disillusion in his voice made her heart ache. His face had gone cold and hard and she was torn between wanting to smooth a hand down his face and tell him it would be okay, and run.

It was odd, because right up until five minutes ago—even three minutes ago—*fear* hadn't come onto her radar with him. "Look, this is going to sound...crazy. I know it does. *I* think it sounds crazy and I'm the one dealing with it. But..." She stopped as she came to the window. Resting a hand on it, she stared into the downpour. Normally, the sound of the rain soothed her. Right then, it sounded ominous. Everything filled her with dread and she couldn't explain it. "I had the worst headache when I woke up this morning. *Everything* hurt. I was trying to do my job and I kept...seeing things. Hearing voices. One of our patients..."

She stopped, licking her lips. "I kept seeing one of our patients. A boy was beating on her. I'd touched her chart while I was trying to scan it and ever since, I couldn't get that idea out of my head. Then I...oh, *shit!*"

She heard a scream and a pale face flashed before her eyes.

"Hailey!"

He stared at her. "Ma'am?"

"Hailey! Hailey... *Fuck,* I can lose my license for this..." Groaning, she shoved a hand through her hair and then swore. "Damn it to hell. Hailey Mullins. She's a patient. I think she's in trouble."

"Ms. Goldman, I'm not in the mood for—"

"Her boyfriend was strangling her!" she shouted it. "I *saw* it."

When he just continued to stare at her, she grabbed her phone. He shot out a hand. "What are you doing?"

"Calling *9-1-1.*"

"And telling them what?" He stared at her as though she'd lost her mind.

She really, really hoped she had.

"I'm going to tell them I heard a scream," she said, improvising. "And give them her address. They're in front of the house."

He grabbed the phone. "You aren't even there."

"Give me the damn phone!" She jerked against his hand, panic flooding her. The pain started to swell in her head and she swung out.

"What the—"

She ended up cuffed, facedown, shuddering, shaking.

"Look, I don't know how you got involved in this, what they are paying you, or what they have on you, but I'm *done.* You're not going to sucker me in—"

His words didn't make any sense. Desperate, she said, "Please...just...you're a fucking cop. Can't you have somebody drive over there? Just *look?* If you're told

31

somebody's in danger, aren't you supposed to do *something*?"

You gullible sack of shit.

Even as he recited the address into his radio, he stared at Nyrene.

His jaw still ached from where she'd clipped him with her elbow. But that was nothing compared to the disgust he felt. At himself.

Because instead of trying to figure out what her angle was and what she knew about Meredith, what was he doing?

His radio chirped and he scowled.

A few minutes later, he stood at the window. Nyrene now sat on the edge of the couch, her hands still cuffed and she was breathing in deep, shuddering gasps.

The uniform—somebody Dev didn't know—said, "Victim is breathing and responsive." He droned on for a few more minutes, but he had nothing else to say that Dev needed to hear.

He'd already heard enough to make his head spin.

Slowly, he turned and looked at Nyrene.

"You want to explain how you knew about that?"

She looked away.

"You've now been connected to two crimes—one murder and one assault. It might have been another dead body," he said, throwing that in when she didn't respond. She flinched and he wanted to kick himself. "So just how did you know what was going on with this girl in the car?"

Finally, she looked at him.

"I saw it," she said, her voice wooden.

"You saw it." He closed his eyes and rubbed the back of his neck. He didn't have the time or the patience for this shit. He was tired and he needed to get about six hours horizontal before he got up and tried to go through the files one more time. There had to be something...

"I *saw* it," she said again, and this time her tone was caustic. "In my *head*. The same way I saw that reporter get shot—only the way it played out in my head *that* time was that you were the one who found her and a couple of cops pounced on you and arrested you."

Dev opened his eyes.

She stared right at him and under the weight of that gaze, he felt something icy trail down his spine.

"And that's not the only thing," she said softly, her lashes sweeping down. "Right before I decided to go to the hospital, I was watching the news...and you were on there."

"What?" Struggling to keep up with this complete and utter insanity, he shook his head. "I was on where—the news?"

"Well, sort of. They were talking about your...death." Now she looked away. "That part got a little blurry— Hey!"

Her skin was soft under his hands. He couldn't help but notice that, just like he couldn't help but notice the fear in her eyes and the way she tried to recoil when he jerked her upright. "You're going to talk," he ground out. "*Who* are you talking to and what do you know?"

"You son of—"

He picked her up and threw her over his shoulder.

Her screech echoed through the house and he grunted as she kicked, managing to drive one knee into his chest before he caught her legs.

A minute later, he found the kitchen and dumped her on a chair.

She stared at him with dumb shock on her face. It hit him like a slap but he ignored it, shoving it down. This was his life he was fighting for, and if she knew something...

Hauling out a chair, he flipped it around until they were face-to-face. "These people are killers. You already know about Meredith," he said, keeping his voice level. "I'm already on their list. You clearly know that. Now *I* am here in your house. Connect the dots, Nyrene. Who do you think is next? They are going to think you talked."

"I don't know what in the hell you're talking about," she said, the words a broken whisper.

"Too late for that."

When she tried to avert her face, he crowded in until he engulfed her field of vision. She shrank back away from him and some small part of him died. Fuck, maybe he should just eat a bullet, get it over with. He'd rather die knowing himself than become a man who was okay crossing the lines he seemed willing to cross lately.

No. He wasn't going to go away that easily. How many good cops, how many decent people, had died because of these fucks? No.

Softening his voice, he leaned in even closer. "You seem like a nice lady, Nyrene. Nice and normal, yet you somehow got caught up in something that's over your head. You really think you get out of this on your own?"

A breath shuddered out of her.

Her pulse slammed away—he could see the rapid beat of it under the thin shield of her skin at the base of her throat. "Meredith thought she could handle herself and look at what happened to her. You want to end up like that?"

A whimper escaped her and she bit her lip to hold back another one, but he caught the faint sound before she muffled it.

He hardened his heart and steeled himself.

"You will, or maybe worse. They just wanted her out of the way. She never made the mistake of getting tangled up with these guys. Now tell me, what do you know and who is it you're talking with?"

He reached up when she lowered her head, brushing her hair back from her face and he discovered it really was as silken as he'd thought. It was a knowledge he didn't need, because one thing was clear—he'd never wrap that hair around his hands, never taste her mouth, never feel her beneath him.

"I'm not working with anybody," she said, her voice soft, almost soundless. "I don't know *what* you're talking about."

"Nyrene—"

"Stop," she said. Slowly, she lifted her head and glared at him. "I already *told* you. I saw it on the fucking news. But it wasn't really there. You were going to be arrested for some sort of corruption shit, and you resisted arrest and you ran. That's what the news report said. Then they gunned you down."

Then she started to laugh, the sound taking on a hysterical edge. "Of course, clearly you're still alive. Maybe I was wrong. Maybe I *wasn't* supposed to warn you earlier. Maybe I was just supposed to let you go. I don't know."

Shaken, he stood, slowly backing away.

She was still laughing, although it sounded more and more like sobs.

She lost track of how long she'd sat there.

It could have been minutes.

It could have been an hour.

But the sound of his shoes—those ugly police shoes—striking the linoleum of her floor made her flinch.

Nyrene hunched her shoulders, wishing she could make herself even smaller, but she couldn't. She'd slammed that mental window shut again, unable to think clearly thanks to all the *other* thoughts in her head. Thoughts that weren't *hers*.

People want him dead. He thinks I'm involved.

The idea terrified her.

He moved behind her. Her breath caught when his hands brushed her wrists.

His hand stilled, for just a moment, and then she heard the clank of metal, her hands freed.

She almost fell on her face in her haste to get away from him. Stumbling over to the far side of the kitchen, she huddled by the back door.

Bennett Deverall stood there, the light shining down on his golden hair and playing with the planes and hollows of his face. He looked as if he'd been born to wear a uniform.

She was officially terrified of him.

He took a step toward her.

She wrapped her arms around herself and started to rock, hating herself for the fear crowding inside her mind. "If you plan on trying to scare me more, do me a favor and just kill me," she said, the words flying out of her mouth before she even knew what she was going to say. "I don't know what you want to hear from me and I don't know what's going on and I..."

He came to a stop in front of her.

Despite her reluctance to look at him, she found herself unable to stand there, hiding her face. Slowly, she shifted her gaze to him and found that the remote stranger who'd taken over for however long he'd been there seem to have faded. No. Not faded.

He was just...restrained.

Once more, his face had a cool politeness. As though he had been simply waiting for her to look at him. He held out a card. "That's my supervisor's name. If you want to file a report, you'll want to talk to him. Talk to *him—*

nobody else, do you understand?"

The urgency in his voice would have worried her. If she wasn't already terrified.

She didn't take the card, though. She just stared at it.

Bennett waited another minute and then leaned over, placing it on the kitchen counter. "I apologize for my actions, Ms. Goldman. I... You should get help for your...headaches."

Get help?

He turned away and she watched him, another hysterical laugh bubbling inside her. Absently, she reached out, brushing the card with her fingers.

The window inside her mind splintered and images leaked through.

"Don't go home." There was a heavy pressure at the base of her skull even as she said the words and picked up the card, stroking it as those images solidified inside her mind. "Don't. They're waiting for you. Don't go home."

Don't.

He'd already come too close to a line and whether she was jerking him around, playing him, or just plain crazy, when he died, he'd rather do it with a clear conscience.

Still, at the doorway to her kitchen, he paused and looked back. "Who's waiting?"

She barely seemed to hear him and she was holding the card that she'd refused to touch only seconds ago. Now her fingers traced it, as if that connection was vital. "Don't go home," she said a third time. "The fire...it touches the sky."

She leaned back against the door, slid down it and just like that, she closed her eyes.

He opened his mouth, closed it. After a minute, he moved closer, prepared to see her flinch, but she didn't do anything, didn't even seem to breathe.

Son of a bitch.

Turning, he strode down the hall, heading to the front door.

He was an idiot.

He was a sucker.

He was going to be dead for it, too, he knew it.

He hit the front door and sixty seconds later, he was

36

gone, speeding away from Nyrene Goldman.

"He's just standing there."

Looking through his binoculars, he watched the big, dark shadow that stood on the balcony overlooking the river.

"Go inside, you stupid fuck."

Bennett Deverall had proven to be a bigger pain in the ass than any of them could have imagined. It had started when he'd gone to double-check on some evidence from a routine traffic stop—one that had turned into a hell of a drug bust for the uniformed cop—and he'd found the report had been altered.

Of course, Deverall *would* keep copies of his reports and he would have a memory like a fucking elephant.

He'd wanted to take him out then.

If he had...

He'd told them that son of a bitch would be trouble. If he'd taken care of him early on, then he wouldn't be sitting out here, listening to the rain pound down on his car while he waited for the stupid shit to go inside.

But all he was doing was sitting on the porch, staring at nothing. After a moment, the man stood and moved to the door.

"Finally..." He started to sigh in relief, but the man turned away *again* and then there was a faint glow. Like a cell phone.

"I'm about ready to come down there and *throw* your ass in the house," he muttered.

Not that he had the option.

This had all been set up in the past couple of hours, but the men he'd chosen were professionals and they were very, very good at what they did.

When this was over, Deverall would be a bad memory and nothing more than a burned corpse to throw into the ground.

He started to worry though as the man began to pace the porch, and he had a sinking suspicion settling in his gut. What if that wasn't Bennett Deverall?

He strained, trying to get a better picture through the binoculars but the man wasn't looking up and with the dark and the rain, it was impossible to tell anything but that he was now talking on the phone.

"This is Deverall."

It was more habit than anything else that had him answering his phone. Staring out at the endless rain, soaked to the bone, he listened to nothing but silence for the first few seconds.

"This is Officer Bennett Deverall. Can I help—"

"You son of a bitch."

The exhaustion from the past day—the past few *months*—cleared as instinct kicked on. "Who is this?"

He didn't expect an answer.

"It's Judd Crowder."

The answer came as if he'd bitten off the words, chewing through steel to say them. Dev closed his eyes. Judd. Meredith's fiancé. She'd been sporting the ring on her broadcasts for the past two months.

"Judd," he said softly. "I'm sorry for—"

"It had something to do with you," Judd said, interrupting. "Didn't it?"

Dev opened his mouth, then closed it. Finally, he fell back on training. "I'm not privy to the details of the investigation, Judd. Have you talked to the investigating officers?"

There was a ragged breath and then Judd said, "No. And I can't. Because I promised her. I've got something for you. I need to see you."

Caution advised against that. The wild grief in Judd's voice told him that it would be a stupid thing to do, meeting with this man right now.

But...

"Look, Deverall. I'm at your house now and I need to give you an SD card. Meredith made me promise if..." His voice broke. "If something happened. Are you going to get your ass here or should I just break down the fucking door?"

"You're at my house?" Dev asked.

"Yeah. So get here before I add breaking and entering, or at least breaking, to my list of experiences."

"Don't—"

It was instinct that had him saying it.

But Judd hung up before the call ended.

38

Don't go in my house, Judd.

He wasn't entirely sure if it had anything at all to do with the utter *bullshit* he'd heard from Nyrene Goldman. Swearing, he jogged back to his car and climbed in. He'd stopped at the small riverfront park a few blocks away, determined to think, determined to clear his head, but if he went home, he'd bury himself in the investigation he'd been conducting on his own.

He was only two blocks from home.

He was close enough to see the explosion—the flames shot up into the air, painting the night a haunting shade of golden orange.

Don't go home...

He hit the gas, but somebody ran in front of him and he hit the brakes just in time to avoid running the man over. "Son of a—"

The gun was pointed right at him.

He looked through the windshield at the man in front of him. While his home burned like an inferno only yards away, he stared down the barrel of a gun.

Jamming his foot on the gas, he ducked low just as the glass of the windshield shattered. He didn't wait to see what happened next. Throwing the car into reverse, he floored it, tires squealing.

He turned the lights off as he whipped the car around and punched it.

He had, literally, only seconds to get away.

If that.

CHAPTER FIVE

"I am telling you—this is a situation we need to look in to."
"*We?*"

The man seated at the table looked up over the rims of the reading glasses he'd slid on. His eyes were blue, his hair blond and his features were GQ perfect. As was the suit he wore. The suit was well made and fit him like a dream and if he'd wanted to, Special Agent in Charge Taylor Jones could turn heads everywhere he went.

And he often did, just not for the reasons people liked.

Now he sighed and leaned back in the chair, crossing his hands over his belly as he studied the woman in front of him. "Taige, unless I'm mistaken, there is no *we* here. You begrudgingly accept cases from me when I think there's a need for you and that's less and less these days. You're now officially wearing Oz's shoes."

His mouth tightened as he glanced away.

The two of them said nothing for a moment and then he looked back at the woman who'd once been his best bloodhound. But she had her own little can of worms now. And his can was much, much bigger.

"I wouldn't be here if I didn't have to be," she said, crossing her arms over her chest. "Trust me, Oz's shoes are damn hard to fill and I'm not even sure I'm equipped. But *I* can't help here."

"If it's riding you this strong—"

She made a disgusted sound. "It's not me, okay?"

Taylor leaned forward. His voice was heavy as he said, "Jillian."

Taige's gaze was grim and she said nothing.

Taylor didn't really need her to, though. The only thing that would have her pushing this hard *was* Jillian.

"Why didn't she call me?" he asked softly.

Taige rubbed her brow. "I've...asked her not to." She moved to the window and stared outside.

Taylor's office was small. Their whole unit was small. Too many people in the Bureau didn't even know Taylor's unit, as it was, existed. On the surface, his was just the standard unit. Under the surface...different story.

He'd clawed and scraped for years to hold this group together, and every year the job got harder. He had meetings, he had cases he was handling himself, and he needed to check in on his people, but the look in Taige's eyes had him rubbing the back of his neck.

"Okay," he said. "Okay. I'll round up Joss. I've got too much here—bureaucratic bullshit—and I can't dodge it. He's the best I can give you."

Blowing out a breath, Taige muttered, "Wonderful."

Taylor lifted a brow.

"I'll just make sure *not* to mention his name to Cullen."

CHAPTER SIX

"We have a problem."

The two cops shared a cup of coffee outside as the older man smoked. "You're a master of understatement."

"No." Blowing out a heavy breath, he looked around, kept the action casual. "This is more than just the clusterfuck with *that* problem."

That problem being the explosion at Deverall's house—one that hadn't killed him. Hard to kill a man when he wasn't even in the damn house.

Should have gone and looked.

Now they had a victim tied to Russell, one who'd busted in the back door of the house. What had Crowder been doing there?

Only one logical explanation, which meant another loose end.

"We've had nothing *but* problems ever since Deverall started looking too closely," he said, lifting his coffee to his lips while the other cop—older than him by twenty years—blew out a smoke ring. "Then that Russell bitch had to get involved. At least she's out of the way."

"We might have another bitch to take her place."

For a moment, he didn't dare breathe. Then, calmly, he put his coffee cup down. "Explain."

"This woman—she's the reason why Deverall didn't show up in the garage the way we'd expected him to." There was a pause, followed by, "Which is *why* Russell shouldn't have been taken out until we had all the pieces we needed."

"I agree." He folded his arms over his chest. "It was a stupid decision and I'll make sure it's rectified—in a way that it can never be repeated." It would take time, but he'd make it happen. "Now, tell me about this new problem. This woman who interfered with our plans for Russell?"

"She was in the ER for a workup. Having trouble getting anybody to talk about her, but my source says she put on quite the show—looked sick out of her head then started having fits, seizure-like. Our good Samaritan"— fury leaked through the otherwise calm voice—"Deverall was on his way out when it started and went to help when it looked like she might get combative. Oddly enough, he was able to smooth things over and she calmed down. Left a few hours later."

"So she got in the way." He shrugged.

"No."

The edge made him look back, studying the man across from him closely.

"It's more complicated. I heard it from the tail I put on Deverall. He was seen at her house last night."

"Who...the woman?" he asked. Disgusted, he turned away and braced his hands on the concrete table in front of him. "If that stupid fuck had waited—"

"He didn't. Now we have to handle her."

He watched as the other cop reached up and rubbed the scar that ran from the corner of his left eye all the way to his jaw. "We got a name?"

The only response was a smile. Nodding, he watched as a couple of uniforms came outside. The mood was grim. Everybody was talking about Deverall, the fire.

"Gas explosion," the youngest of the uniforms said. "So far, that's what people are talking about. I know it's early yet, but a gas explosion?"

As the men lit up a few feet down, he pretended to chat with his friend—the two of them were detectives, had been on the force for years, and while they were friendly enough with the uniforms they never bothered to strike up conversations.

He listened for a few more minutes as he pretended to enjoy the rest of his coffee break.

Then the two of them went in. As they parted ways, his friend clapped a hand on his back. "Don't let that young partner of yours drive you too crazy today, man."

They shared a grim look.

"He's not that bad. You get back to me if anything

pops on that case, or the new female suspect."

The words were vague, but they both received the messages loud and clear.

"You look better than you did yesterday."

Nyrene glanced at Michelle over her cup of coffee as she stared at the morning news.

You tried.

She'd only told herself that twenty times since she'd seen the report. It wasn't having any more effect now than it had the first twenty times.

"I feel better," she said vaguely, aware Michelle was still watching her.

She did. Physically. Except for the nausea that gripped her now as she watched the news unfolding on the TV. There was less noise in her head now, but if she let her focus drop, that window would inch open and noise and images would overtake her thoughts.

"Terrible, isn't it? That guy was a war hero," Michelle said softly. "I read about him. His unit was under attack. Like eight or nine men were injured and they were cornered. He held the attackers off until more help came. And now this..."

Nyrene closed her eyes, turning away from the skeletal remains of the wall. That was all that was left.

"At this time, we have no new information..." The sober-eyed brunet stared grimly into the camera for a moment before looking back at the devastation of the house behind him. "The Clary Police Department asks that anybody with information contact them."

He read off the number as it was displayed on the screen.

Nyrene resisted the urge to laugh hysterically. *Hi. I tried to tell him not to go inside...*

"The jerk is here," Michelle said.

Nyrene glanced over as the bright red convertible pulled into the parking lot. Dr. Evered—Dr. Evil—climbed out a moment later, talking on his phone, his perpetually grouchy face looking grouchier than ever.

"Did he give you much grief yesterday?" she asked as they left the break room. The rest of the staff was up front. There were only two nurses in the back, although one of the front office works had medical assistant training and could help in a pinch.

"Surprisingly, no." Michelle grinned. "Of course, I started it off by saying 'she pretty much passed out in the office.' I think he'd just as soon you not do anything that could mess up his plans to get out of here and move to Puerto Vallarta or wherever he wants to go. Suing his ass would probably do it."

Nyrene didn't respond.

She couldn't stop thinking about the news report.

The house.

And the way Bennett Deverall had looked.

He'd terrified her, yes.

She still had the card he'd given her. She hadn't called his supervisor. Even if she hadn't heard the news today, she wouldn't have.

Another image of the house's husk flashed through her memory and she ducked into a room, rested her head against the glass.

When she opened her eyes, she started to scream.

* * * * *

"I am telling you—I *saw* somebody."

Nyrene sat in the back of the office, two cops towering over her. One of them sighed and sat in the chair in front of her. "Ma'am." Then he smiled, a charming smile that set off the dimple in his chin. "May I call you Nyrene? It's a lovely name."

She just stared at him. His name was Detective Morehead. He was a few years older than she was and the more talkative of the two partners. The older cop, Morehead's partner, introduced himself as Lieutenant Larry Oman, but he let the younger cop take control.

And that was exactly what Morehead did, guiding the conversation, asking questions, being a pushy bastard, but he hid it behind a mask of faux concern.

"I believe you think you saw something," he said, and he leaned forward. His eyes were compassionate. His body language nonthreatening.

But everything in Nyrene told her to *run*. Or maybe that was just the fear screaming inside her. She didn't think so, though. Something about Morehead creeped her the hell out.

It bubbled up into her voice. "You don't under*stand,*" she said, her voice breaking. "This is like the th-third time in just a couple of days this has happened to me. I see somebody..."

She stopped, swallowing the words back. They'd think she was crazy, if they didn't already.

"Look, I *saw* somebody," she said. "*Bodies*—two men standing over a woman. One of them..."

The image coalesced, then solidified in her mind, and she reached up, trailed one finger down her cheek. "One of them had a scar. She was..."

"A scar?"

Oman flipped open a little notebook, drawing her eyes to him. He was a middle-aged man, average height, with brown hair that was quickly going to gray. His eyes were pure cop and he didn't bother to hide his skepticism as he commented, "That's impressive that you could see that from so far away."

"It was like I was right there," she murmured, but now she had to doubt.

How had she seen that scar?

It was a couple dozen yards down from the office where she worked and what she'd seen. They'd been between the cars, staring down at the woman.

"What did she look like?" Oman asked.

"I don't know." Nyrene swallowed. "I didn't see her face. Just her clothes—scrubs."

"Scrubs?"

She plucked at her black pants. "Like these. Hers were dark. A red top, like mine."

The image swam before her eyes—became clearer. And that vicious pain started in the back of her head. *Oh, no...oh, no...*

"I...um." She licked her lips. "I think I need to sit down. I'm not feeling well."

"Ma'am...you are sitting down."

She lurched up out of the seat. "I have to go."

Oman reached the door before she did. "Are you all right, Ms. Goldman?"

No. Yes. Hysterical laughter bubbled in the back of her throat, because that image was *right there* now—in living color and clear as day. In her mind, and only in her mind.

She'd seen somebody all right. Only what she'd seen hadn't happened yet.

Just like she'd been doing for days.

"I'm fine," she said with a weak smile. "I've just had a rough couple of days. A car wreck, then...this. Can we...can we do this later? I mean, you all didn't see anybody..."

"Of course." Morehead moved to join them. "Here's my card. Call when you're ready to go over this." He paused and then added, "We'll take a look around, though. Make sure we don't see anything suspicious."

"Of course."

"I'm so sorry."

It was well after five when they'd cleared their crazy, full schedule of patients. Point to him—it was also Friday, so he'd managed to ruin her weekend, too.

She had to give Dr. Evil credit. He'd worked her ass off for more than nine hours. Well, more like six and a half since she'd had to deal with the mess from the cops. That had added to the insanity of the day.

She was now jobless. Evered had fired her only minutes ago.

Gathering up her things, Nyrene tried to smile at Michelle. "We know how he is. We could be bleeding from the eyes and he'd want to know why there was red on his charts."

So he'd fired her.

She'd find another job.

Go home.

Walk out there in the parking lot...

Abruptly, a weight fell off her shoulders. She'd seen it happen *here*. If she wasn't here, then it couldn't happen. "And I'm not wearing red today," she added.

"What? Red?"

"Nothing. Gallows humor," she said as she looked down at the box. It held so little, but Evered hadn't been one to encourage any kind of attachments in the workplace.

"Call me," Michelle said.

"I'll will."

With a deep, shaky sigh, she headed out the back door

of the office for the last time. The bank of elevators was empty and she jabbed at a button.

Today called for the ice cream session to end all ice cream sessions.

If he'd gotten there two minutes later, he would have missed them.

Now, as he crouched inside the van parked next to Oman and Morehead, Bennett Deverall held his breath and waited. He'd shown up to keep an eye on her, talk to her, ask her...*something*...when he'd caught some chatter over the scanner. He'd left his radio, but Dev knew a thing or two and had a way with computers.

Almost any idiot with a laptop could figure out how to listen to the police scanner these days, but it took a little more to listen in on conversations.

It was child's play for him.

He didn't know *what* he was looking for, or doing, but his gut told him he needed to get more information from Nyrene Goldman and when he'd heard her name go out on the scanner, he'd gone to the address listed.

He'd watched from the parking garage as two of the cops he'd worked with climbed out of their squad car and strode toward the building. They'd parked in the fire lane, right next to the parking for the disabled and when the elderly woman and her daughter had taken the parking space just a few feet away, Dev had told himself he wouldn't do anything.

Then he heard the daughter complain about how long they'd be there, the mother's apologetic murmur. They'd be inside for a while...

He'd jimmied the locks without a qualm.

It probably wouldn't do him any good, but he had to take the chance.

Through the windshield, Dev watched as Oman and Morehead exited the building. Although nobody could have seen much of anything in this dark, worn old van, Dev slunk lower down and tugged on the brim of his ball cap.

And he listened.

"...bitch knows something, I'm telling you," Morehead said.

"Leave it alone," Oman said. "It's already hot enough right now, with Russell gone, and the botched job from last night. We can't risk getting close to another connection to him."

"And if *she* can somehow pass on information?"

There was a pause and then Oman said softly, "You heard me."

The words were mild.

The tone wasn't.

Dev didn't have a chance to hear anything else because the door slammed shut a minute later.

Through his teeth, he whistled and then eased forward, watching from the shrouded shadows of the van until the detective and lieutenant disappeared.

Now, just what had they been talking to Nyrene about?

"Hi."

Nyrene bumped into the big, rough-looking bastard on her way out the door.

"Excuse me," she said.

He just smiled. "I'm trying to locate one of the offices here...Dr. Evered? You work here?"

"I did." She nodded toward the elevator bank. "Up to the third floor, go right. But they've already closed for the day."

"That's fine." He gave her a wide, easy smile. It was full of warmth—the kind that might have made her heart flutter if it hadn't felt like it was breaking all day. "I'm just looking for a new doctor, was going to grab whatever paperwork. I'll just come back tomorrow."

With a vague smile, she went to go around him.

"Hey, is this yours?"

She glanced down.

Somebody bumped into the man in front of her and he steadied her with a hand on her arm.

Her brain seemed to gray out on her for just a second—

Then she jerked back.

No. She wasn't taking any more chances with people touching her. No more. No more. She wanted to wrap herself in bubble wrap and never touch *anything* again.

"Ah..." She eyed the business card he held in front of

him. "Mine?"

"Yeah. It just fell on the floor." Brown eyes bore into hers. "Is it yours?"

Without thinking, she reached out and snatched it, shoving it in her purse. "Thanks. Good luck with the doctor." Then she cut around him and headed through the automatic doors.

It wasn't quite six, but the days were getting shorter and the cloudy day cast everything in a grim, dark light. Or maybe that was her. As she hurried to her car, she looked around. She wouldn't be coming back. Automatically, her gaze moved to the spot where she'd seen the woman in her...dream? Vision?

Whatever it was that was going on. She didn't know and part of her didn't *care*. She wanted it to stop.

And right then, she just wanted to get in her car...

She slowed to a halt.

Her car.

It was right by...

She swept her gaze to the light post on the passenger side. She'd always parked there because of the light. The big truck next to it seemed to take up two spaces and there was a van almost as big in the parking space in front. She could barely see her car, but that was where...

Stop freaking yourself out.

She hurried to her car, still clutching the box.

"Ms. Goldman."

She stopped, startled as somebody moved out from behind the big truck.

"Oh...ah, Detective Morehead, right?" She gave him a tight smile.

The scuff of a shoe on pavement behind her had her glancing back.

She didn't see the blow coming until it was too late.

CHAPTER SEVEN

"Hurry." Troy Morehead grabbed her before she would have gone to the ground.

The man in front of him—a kid really—moved forward and jerked open the side door of the supply truck. Darnell Hampton was a seventeen-year-old dropout with fists the size of hammers and lots of greed. Troy had been using him for information...and other things...for going on three years now.

"This is *stupid*, man," Darnell said, bending to grab the woman's feet. His face was twisted in a scowl, the scar that ran from his temple to the corner of mouth paler against his dark skin.

"Be quiet and move. You ride in the back. If she causes any trouble, cut her open."

Darnell swore. "Anybody can walk—"

The click behind Morehead had them both freezing.

"You want to put her down now?"

Morehead stared at Darnell. Darnell's eyes flitted to the gun and he licked his lips.

As the muzzle of a gun pushed hard against the bone just behind Morehead's ear, Officer Bennett Deverall asked again, "You want to put her down? It's going to get really messy if I put a bullet in you."

"Come on now, Dev," Morehead said, his mind racing furiously.

"You heard me."

Morehead gave a short nod. He needed his hands to act. "Drop her," he said.

And he did just that, right before he spun. Darnell took off running.

A fist caught Morehead in the gut with all the strength of a sledgehammer. Air blasted out of him and he didn't even have a chance to suck in more oxygen to replace it before he was thrown up against the truck, a heavy forearm at his throat.

"Hey there, Dev," he managed to squeeze out.

Dev leaned in, the gun still in his hand. He jammed it into Morehead's side. "Now...just what were you going to do with her?"

"Ah. You know. Dates are hard to find these days." He had to get to his—

A scream split the air.

Dev shoved back just as a woman, face pale and eyes wide, ran away from where she'd glimpsed them between the truck and the van.

Morehead went for his weapon.

"Do it and you die now," Dev said, backing up out of reach. He had his Glock trained on Morehead in an easy, two-handed grip and his gaze was unwavering.

"You don't want to kill a cop, man."

"Yeah? I don't want to *be* killed, either. Funny how none of you seem to give a shit about that." Dev's lips twitched. "Back away...*now.*"

Slowly, he did, casting the girl one last look.

His mind whirled.

He had to fix this.

He already knew people were gunning for him because of the fuck-up with Russell. Had to fix it.

As Dev went to one knee, he let his hand hang looser.

"Don't," Dev said, his voice gentle. "I'll put a dozen holes in you before you hit the ground. You won't even know you're dead. Now. You just keep right on moving. Back up, back up..."

Dev had no idea where the man came from.

One minute he'd been preparing himself to kill a fellow cop, or at least wound him, and the next, Morehead was jerked off his feet, disappearing between the van and the truck.

A man, easily as big as Dev, appeared in the next moment, holding Morehead off his feet while the cop struggled against the choke hold.

"Go," the man said. "*Now.*"

"What..."

"Don't make me say it again." His gaze flicked to the woman and something that looked like regret appeared.

"I'm not leaving her," Dev warned.

"Did I ask you to? Now *move.*"

He didn't wait another second. Hefting her in his arms, he picked up the keys and the bag she'd dropped and unlocked her car, dumping her into the back. Her purse fell onto the floor as he slammed the door shut.

He was in the front and whipping out of the space a few seconds later.

By the time the first cops arrived on scene through the main entrance, he was calmly driving out the other, ball cap turned backward, sunglasses on.

And an unconscious woman in the back of the car.

This hadn't gone as planned.

He flicked a glance in the rearview mirror at the sound of the low moan.

"You waking up back there?" he asked as another cop car blasted by him.

"Unghh..."

The muffled grunt had him grimacing. That kid who'd hit her—he'd been a giant, easily three or four inches taller than Dev, and Dev stood six four.

"Come on, Nyrene," he said, keeping his voice level as he pulled into a parking garage a few blocks from the hospital. Had to get out of this car. Now.

He yanked open the back door just as she was sitting up.

She caught sight of him and jerked back, all but cringing against the door on the far side.

"Get out of the car," he said.

"No." It came out as a tight whisper.

Fuck. He bent down, one hand braced on the hood, the other on the door. "In about five minutes, this whole block is going to be shut down, if not sooner. You just had a cop try to kill you. I'm the *only* reason you're not dead right now." Okay, that might be exaggeration, but he as pretty sure Morehead hadn't been about to throw her into that moving truck just because he wanted to discuss her choice in uniform wear.

Her dazed eyes cleared as she blinked. "The... I saw the

detective," she whispered.

"Yeah. You did. Congratulations, you're now on his shitlist, too. Now...think again before you tell me no."

He wasn't proud of himself when she climbed out.

He'd scared her into it.

"Wait," she whispered, the words choked.

"No time."

She jerked back and stretched out her hand, grabbing the heavy red bag he'd dumped into the car with her.

Swearing, he slammed the door shut and they moved down the aisle.

"Don't speak," he warned as they came to a stop beside a beige sedan. Boring as hell. Perfect. He had the door open in seconds and unlocked her door. "Get in."

"You... This isn't your car."

"No."

She said nothing else for the next twenty minutes.

They stopped at a shopping mall just off the interstate and he left the sedan there, watching the crowds moving in and out of the mall.

"I can't believe you want to see that movie again," an indulgent voice said.

He tuned in on it and watched as a couple moved away from a black Ford Escape. It was an older model, clean. No dents or anything that made it stand out.

And...

"Look at it this way," the guy said, tugging the girl up against him. "It doesn't start for another forty-five minutes. You got all that time in the bookstore."

Perfect.

He waited until they were through the main entrance and then he got to work.

"You're stealing another car," she said, her voice faint.

"Yes."

"You're a cop."

Grimly, he said, "Trust me, I know."

They got on the road again and didn't stop for two hours. The lights of New Orleans gleamed in the night as he backed into a parking space on a crowded level of the garage.

"Another car?" she asked.

"No. We're keeping this one for a while. I just need to do one quick thing."

It wouldn't be long before the SUV was reported stolen. Swapping out the plates wouldn't buy them a lot of time, but it would give him a little longer to think.

Once he slid back into the vehicle, he looked over at Nyrene. The left side of her face was a vicious, ugly, mottled black and blue. He should have gotten her some ice—something.

"How's your head?"

She huddled deeper into the seat, staring out the window.

"Nyrene?"

"What's going on?" she asked softly.

"As soon as you start telling me the truth, we can start to figure that out." He shrugged and put the Escape into drive.

"I did."

He opened his mouth to say something—anything— and decided not to. Not then.

They needed to get some food, and while he was reasonably certain the scruffy clothes, his haggard face and the light growth of beard he'd developed over the past two days would alter his appearance some, it wasn't enough and there were too many cops here, too many cameras.

The bigger city was ideal for what he needed—Clary wasn't a small town, but it wasn't big, either. Swapping out plates back there wouldn't do him much good when cops started eyeballing every vehicle, looking for him.

By now, they had a BOLO out for him but he was hoping the anonymity of the city would work on his side for a short while. As he pulled out onto the street, he said softly, "Here's the deal, Nyrene. I pissed off the wrong people in Clary. I've known it for a while and I was ready to deal with what happened. Bad cops—"

"Bad cops?" She stiffened.

"That wasn't the tooth fairy you ran in to at your work," he said, his voice grim.

She sucked in a breath.

"Corruption," she whispered. Then she swore. "I am an *idiot.*"

"Naive, at the very least," he agreed. "Getting involved with men like Morehead, what did you think would happen?"

"Morehead?"

He glanced over at her just as she straightened and leveled a glare at him. "I got involved with *you*, you jackass. All of this started when I tried to warn you not to go into that garage!"

"About that." He nodded, grimacing at the slow-moving traffic all around. Absently, he hit the locks on the doors and the safety that kept her from unlocking her door. "How did you know about Meredith?"

She didn't respond.

The light turned red and he slowed to a stop, turning his gaze on her once more. "She was just doing her job. She hadn't hurt anybody. She didn't deserve to die like that." He paused, saw the tears forming in her eyes and pushed. "She was engaged to a nice guy. They would have been married in another four months."

She sucked in a breath.

Bastard.

"Who told you about her? How did you get involved in this?"

Nyrene felt the threads of her temper snap. Her head was hurting—no. Not her head, her *face*. She'd caught a glimpse of her reflection and she looked like she'd gone one-on-one with a pro boxer...and she'd lost.

She'd left her car in a parking garage.

She had nothing more than her purse, the cash and laptop inside it, and that was about it.

Bennett sighed, the sound almost bored, as if he could keep this up all night. "I already told you, I can't start to help you until you tell me what's going on."

"You want to know?" she asked, the words escaping her in a rush. She twisted around to glare at him.

He had a faint smile on his face. He checked the mirror and then hit the entrance ramp to the freeway, merging into traffic. She couldn't decide what she hated more, the faint smirk he wore now or the scary son of a bitch she'd faced last night.

"I hit my head." She said it slowly. "In the wreck, I hit my head. The headache got worse and worse. I kept hearing *voices*..."

She paused and reached up, hitting her temple with the heel of her hand. It sent a sickening wave of pain through her, but she ignored it. "I'd hear whispers and mutters and yells and screams and I *couldn't shut them up.* The next day, I was watching the news and I saw *you.* You were *dead.* The headline? *Local officer, celebrated war hero Bennett Deverall was gunned down.*"

His hands tightened on the steering wheel. "That's their plan?"

"You stupid son of a bitch!" she shouted. "I don't know who *they* are. I saw this!"

She grabbed her hair and tugged, ignoring the pain it sent splintering through her. Her face pounded from where she'd been hit, but she was almost inured to the agony now. "I *saw* it in my *head.* You dense idiot! I saw it..." Her voice broke and she looked away. Cold now, the fury suddenly gone, she drew up her knees. "Just like I saw them kill her. It was in my head...just in my head."

* * * * *

"Agent Crawford, you want to tell me again just why you assaulted one of my officers?"

Joss kept his smile in place and stared at the cop in front of him. Damn, but it was a mess here.

The captain, who'd settled down in front of him, had a hard expression to her face. She was probably a few years older than she seemed. He imagined she'd have to be. She barely appeared old enough to be in her twenties, but in order for her to be a captain, she'd have to be double that.

Good bone structure, he decided.

The grim look in her eyes made up for the somewhat youthful appearance though. She had a cop's gaze on her and he'd bet his right nut she was a good cop.

Captain Clair Amana didn't look like the kind of woman who'd take a lot of shit, but unfortunately, she was running a department full of it and it didn't sit well on her.

Joss had figured all of that out within a few seconds of shaking the hand of one Clair Amana, thanks to a little hook-up with Taige Morgan. His abilities might be a freak show among freak shows, but the chameleon act, the gift that let him pick up any other psychics, made this a lot easier to figure out.

If he was going to wade into a nest of snakes, he

wanted to know how big the nest was.

The cop he'd grabbed in the parking lot was as dirty as they came.

The cop who'd shown up on the scene ten minutes later, also dirty.

There was a uniform who'd escorted him into the captain's office and yeah, he was dirty, but he was also scared. Joss had caught images of a woman's face in his mind—a woman, with a gun pressed to her head.

He didn't have time to think through all the shit he was picking up, and he wasn't used to working it like Taige was. It would take him a while.

But it was good to be in a room with a cop who wasn't dirty.

"I already explained this," Joss said with a sigh. "I saw him going for his weapon."

"He has a different story."

Scraping his nails down his chin, Joss shrugged. "Well, I can't help that. I saw a man going for a gun. I had about two seconds to assess the situation and all I could see was the woman on the ground and a man kneeling in front of her. He looked like he was trying to help."

"Detective Morehead tells me Officer Deverall had a gun on her."

Liar. "No." Joss shook his head. "That's not what it looked like. He was the one on his knees trying to help. Honestly, I was surprised as hell when your man told me he was a cop. He hadn't declared himself, issued any sort of warning..."

He wasn't surprised to see the flash in the back of Captain Amana's gaze. *You know something's going on, don't you?*

Joss thought about trying to touch her again, see if he could pick up something, but his job wasn't this town, or their problems. His *job* could be halfway to Toronto by now and he was on his ass, making nice with the locals.

"Just what brings you to Clary, Agent Crawford?"

"Visiting." Without a blink, he lied and said, "My wife and I are looking to relocate out of DC. I might have the chance to move to the Nashville office but I wanted to get the lay of the land."

"Nashville, huh?" Amana cocked her head. A wisp of blonde hair escaped from her ponytail, falling down to frame her face. "That would be a commute from here to Clary. Something of a step down, I'd think, too, going from the capitol to Tennessee."

"My wife hates big cities." He shrugged and said it easily, although Dru would rather eat raw chicken before moving to a small town—*I feel claustrophobic*, she'd told him when they'd gone back home to visit his folks.

Instead of answering, Amana picked up the card Joss had given her.

"Okay." She tapped the edge of it on her desk and then nodded toward the door. "I'll have a talk with my detective, Agent."

Joss didn't wait another second before he hauled ass out of there.

It rubbed him raw, though, walking out of what felt like a nest of vipers.

Because he took his pleasures where he could, he gave Detective Morehead a mock salute on his way out the door. "I'll be seeing you around, Detective."

If he didn't know better, he would have almost believed her.

Almost.

Dev fought to keep his expression relaxed, even his hands loose and easy on the steering wheel as he navigated the light traffic on the interstate. It was late, and getting later, but it would be another hour before they made it to where he wanted to go.

He had that one hour to figure out just what in the hell he was going to do with a woman who was at the same time, beautiful, frustrating...and either the best damn liar he'd ever met or completely and utterly crazy.

He couldn't let her go back to Clary.

That much was certain. No matter how she'd gotten involved in this, he couldn't believe the scared, quiet woman at his side had gotten involved with the scum of the earth because she wanted to.

Her breathing was getting slower, steadier and after a few more minutes, he chanced a look over. The dim light coming from the dashboard was barely enough for him to make out her face, but her lashes were low over her eyes.

If she wasn't asleep, then she was pretty close to it.

No. She wasn't involved in this because she wanted to be—that took a certain sort of mindset, a certain type of person. If she was that kind of person, then she'd know better than to fall asleep in the cab of the truck with him.

His phone started to vibrate and he tugged it from his pocket, gave it a quick look.

Amana's number came up and he had to resist the urge to hurl the phone out the window. He needed to get rid of it, should have done it already.

"Ummm..."

A soft, throaty sigh came from across the bench seat and he bit back a groan as his blood heated in response. He could imagine her making that sigh as he spread her out beneath him...

Not happening.

Spying an exit up ahead, he hit his blinker. He needed coffee and a couple of minutes away, out of the SUV. The whole damn vehicle smelled like her now and it wasn't helping him think anymore.

"What..."

He set his jaw, prepared for the questions, the accusations, the pleas.

She just cleared her throat. "What are we doing?"

"I need coffee and the tank's running low."

Slowly, she straightened up in the seat, wincing as she stretched. The action pushed her breasts against the thin cotton of her scrubs top—it was a pale pink that warmed against the gold of her skin. Not that he could see it now, but he'd seen her too well earlier. Seen her enough to imprint the look of her forever on his brain, and his libido kept taunting him with images of how it would be to peel those utilitarian scrubs from her body, how soft her skin would be, how full and heavy her breasts would feel in his hands.

Her breath hitched in her throat and he glanced at her from the corner of his eye, wondering if she'd caught the same heavy tension in the air—

But she was pale.

Her gaze locked, almost blindly, on the oasis of light up ahead. "Don't," she whispered.

"What?"

She shook her head and sank deeper, lower into the seat. "Don't stop there."

The odd note in her voice—the same one he'd heard when she'd lain on the floor in the ER, the same one he'd heard when she'd told him not to go home—was back and he wanted to slam his fist into the steering wheel.

"Nyrene," he said, keeping his voice flat. "I've had enough of the bullshit. I don't know what you *think* is going on in your head, but whatever it is, get over it. We're stopping."

"There's somebody there." She spun her head around, her eyes huge in her face. "You can't stop. Not here."

"There's nobody there!" he snapped, wrenching on the steering wheel with more force than he needed. They took the sharp exit too fast and he sucked in a breath as she was shoved back up against the door. *Damn it*. He had to get his head together. Why was she getting to him like this?

He clenched his jaw. "I'm sorry..." Blowing out a breath, he said, "Nobody has been following us, nobody knows what we're driving and there's no way anybody could be here—"

She made a lunge for the steering wheel and jerked it. He swore.

And then he swore again as he grabbed her and shoved her head down—the glass had exploded as the bullet went through the windshield, catching it right at the edge. Glass rained down all over them.

"Son of a *bitch*!" Instinct kicked in even as some part of his mind wanted to draw back. *How...what...that...*

He was babbling inside his own mind.

There was another voice up there chatting, too. One that stood back and calmly analyzed what had just happened. It had taken into account the direction of the vehicle, where the bullet had slammed into the windshield—

If she hadn't grabbed the wheel, you'd be without most of your head right now, son.

Dev ignored both voices as he whipped the truck into reverse and spun around, tearing out of the parking lot so fast the tires squealed.

Had to move. Get back on the expressway, although, *damn it*, how far would he get with the windshield busted like this?

"Don't..."

She sucked in a breath. "Don't take the expressway."

"No choice," he said grimly. "We're sitting ducks on a road this quiet."

"No...don't...take the expressway."

Instinct warred with reason, and at the very last moment, he whipped the steering wheel around and punched it, taking them flying off into the night, away from the truck stop. The illusion of solitude was shattered moments later when two, then three, sets of headlights came boiling out of the parking lot and headed toward them.

"Left."

"Do you know where the fuck we are?" he snarled. "There's no road!"

"Go...left." She slumped deeper in the seat, her hands fisted in her hair.

He crested the slight swell. His brain processed the four-way stop. He didn't slow down, just turned left and once more hit the gas. "I hope you know these roads, Nyrene."

It twisted and snaked around and the cars behind them were closing in. Dev could drive with the best of them, but the SUV wasn't built for this kind of driving.

"Train."

He barely heard her, too busy trying to figure out what to do, how to do it, when—

"Train!" she shouted.

The tracks...

He saw the RR crossing coming up out of the darkness. *There's not going to be a train...*

But there was, speeding down on them. He shoved the gas pedal to the floor. They busted through the heavy, striped arm that had just lowered and cleared the tracks.

He chanced a look off into the darkness and saw the long, unending line of the train stretching off into the north. "How the hell did you...?"

He clamped his mouth shut over the rest of the question and focused on one thing. Driving.

That train wouldn't last forever.

They needed a new vehicle and they needed to get out of the open.

Just beyond the train speeding by, he could see the cars that had come to a halt.

Son of a bitch. He reached down and picked up the

phone, taking a second to study the screen. Amana hadn't called again, but she'd sent two texts.

You need to get in touch with me. Now.

The second one had a grimmer tone.

Damn it, Deverall, where the fuck are you?

Without letting himself think about it, he threw the phone out the window.

He still hadn't gotten his damn coffee.

CHAPTER EIGHT

It was nearly one in the morning when Nyrene found herself standing in a small cabin, one that seemed lost in the middle of nowhere.

The past few hours were just a blur.

They'd stopped at a busy motel off the interstate some hours back and her body had almost cried in relief.

But they hadn't been there to get a room and she'd figured that out when he had her wait for him at the edge of the parking lot, in a shadowy area on the other side of the building from where they'd left the truck with its busted window. He'd parked with the broken windshield facing away from the rest of the vehicles and he'd knocked the rest of the glass out earlier as they drove.

She'd stood there, feeling lost and clutching her purse as he prowled around, clearly searching for something. She hadn't been able to figure out what until they were pulling out of the paid parking lot. He'd used cash—twenty dollars he'd pulled out of his pocket and then they were gone.

He tossed the ticket stub down in the console. It read *Park & Fly.*

"Hopefully the car's owner will be gone for a few days. Give us a bit of a breather," he'd said.

A breather.

She thought about that now and wondered just how she was supposed to breathe past the band fear had wrapped around her chest, around the knot that seemed to be permanently lodged in her throat.

"We'll be safe here for a couple of days," Dev told her. Then his eyes narrowed. "Unless you know something I don't."

She looked at him as he stood in the doorway separating the two rooms of the cabin. "What?"

"How did they find us?"

Damn it. Tears choked her as she lifted her face to the ceiling. "I don't *know.*"

"I don't get it. Explain to me— Just *explain* how you could have gotten— Son of a bitch." He shoved off the wall and came toward her. "Give me your bag."

She stared at him for a second before lowering her gaze to the vivid pink purse she carried. "My...my bag?"

He didn't bother to ask again, just reached for it and she lost the tug of war, a sob bubbling out of her as he upended it and started to go through it.

He threw her laptop on the floor.

"Would you be careful with that?" she half-shouted. "That's my—"

He gave her a dark look.

She sucked in a breath as he looked away, going through everything that had come tumbling out of her purse. He pushed aside a couple of tampons, a brush, the loose change and the lipstick she never remembered to put on. Then he stopped and went back, picking up the lipstick and taking the cap off, twisting it up.

"It's not your color," she said, the words popping out of her before she could stop them.

He ignored her, continuing his scrutiny of the tube of lipstick. When he got to her phone, she snidely said, "It's not on. My ex-boss hates cell phones. I keep it off and never got around to turning it on, seeing as how I was being knocked unconscious and then dragged halfway across the state."

A muscle in his jaw twitched as he swiped the screen, but it remained dark. Without saying anything, he popped off the back and took out the battery and the SIM card.

He dropped the phone and smashed it under his boot.

"When was the last time you called anybody?"

She glared at him.

"When was the last time you called anybody?" he asked again, his voice level, the words patient. But his eyes were freaking intense and she had to keep her feet all but glued in place as he took a step toward her.

"At the hospital."

"Who did you call?"

65

"A cab." Wrapping her arms around herself, she fought the urge to shiver. *Reaction*, she thought. It was reaction. She wasn't cold, but she was exhausted and hungry and half-sick with the fear.

"Where were you going?"

"*Seriously?*" Her jaw fell open as she stared at him. "Did you *see* me yesterday? I went *home*."

"And did...?"

"I called over some guys I know and we had a three-way on my kitchen table," she said.

His heavy chest moved under the faded cotton of the T-shirt he wore—black with a faded *AC/DC* logo on it. He'd kept a light gray warm-up jacket on over it earlier, but he'd taken it off, left it hanging on the back of the chair. Now she could see the gun the jacket had concealed, tucked in a shoulder holster of some sort under his left arm.

Her gaze locked on it, unable to move, even when he moved closer.

"Don't make me keep asking these questions, Nyrene," he said. "I'm tired. You are, too. The sooner I figure this out, the sooner we can find something to eat and get some rest."

In response to the word *eat*, her stomach rumbled. She'd managed a piece of toast for breakfast, but after she'd seen the news about his house, she hadn't been able to eat anything.

"See?"

She tore her gaze away from the gun and looked at him. He had an amused smile on his lips. "You're hungry, too. Just help me out here. What did you do yesterday...other than your three-way?"

Blood rushed to her cheeks and she moved away, cutting a wide berth around him. Stopping at the window, she stared out into the darkness. She had no idea where they were. The hours of driving, the several stops and starts, the times they'd switched cars—all of it blurred together, turning the day into nothing but a surreal haze.

In all honesty, nothing had felt entirely real since she'd started getting these headaches.

The damn wreck.

Wood creaked and she jerked her head up. She gasped as it sent a jolt of pain through her and she whimpered, bringing her hands up to cradle her head. When she touched the left side of her face, she flinched.

The pain there seemed to merge, blending with every other part of her body that hurt.

A hand touched her arm and she twisted away. "Don't," she said, squeezing the words out.

Tucking her back against the wall, she waited for the wave of misery to fade before making herself look at him.

That implacable expression was on his face.

"I laid down. I felt awful. I tried to sleep and couldn't. So I got on my computer." She glanced over at it, thought of the website she'd visited, the email—

Her hands clenched into fists.

He moved toward it and she managed to keep her face blank as he picked it up, putting it on the table. "Is there any kind of LoJack software on this?"

"What?" She stared at him.

He rubbed his temple and for that one moment, he looked as tired and frustrated as she felt. Although she saw no sign of the *terror* on his rugged features. "LoJack software, something to track it?"

"No." She rubbed her arms, the chill returning as his gaze came back to her.

He studied her for a minute and then shook his head. "Can't take the chance. I have to—"

"No!" She lunged at him, wrapping her hands around it, her fear forgotten, her terror. Everything, but the need to get that computer away from him. "Give it to me. There's nothing—"

He ripped it away, her desperate grip no deterrent to the savage strength in him. "Enough!"

He hurled it onto the couch and caught her arms. "That's enough! Don't you get it? I've got people trying to kill me and now they are probably after you. You need to tell me what is going on, how they are tracking us and how they managed to be at the fucking truck stop when I didn't even know I was going to be there."

He glared at her, blue eyes viciously bright in the dim light. His hands gripped her arms with terrifying strength. Her toes barely touched the ground.

His face was just inches from her own.

It was completely insane that her response was laughter. Hysterical, awful little giggles that made her own ears hurt to hear it, but she couldn't stop.

Slowly, his grip on her arms loosened.

Her feet touched the floor and he let go. She sagged to the floor, off balance, and the only thing that kept her from falling was the return of his hands to her arms.

"Son of a bitch," he muttered.

He half-carried her over to the couch and deposited her there, eying her narrowly as she continued to laugh.

"You..." she whispered after long, horrid moments. Her throat felt raw and her cheeks were wet.

At some point, the laughter had turned to sobs and she didn't even remember when it happened.

"You stupid ass." Utterly drained, she let her head drop onto the back of the couch, and stared desolately at her laptop. Half of her life—just about all her hopes for a future—were tied up in that computer.

And if he decided to destroy it, she couldn't stop him.

"You stupid ass," she said again. "I don't know how they found us. I don't know who *they* are."

Wrapping her arms around her middle, she sank deeper into the cushions of the couch. "But I already told you what was going on. You just didn't want to listen. Not yesterday...and not now. I don't know what else to tell you."

"What's on the computer?" Dev's gut twisted into vicious, ugly knots. He needed to walk away from her— walk away, make something to eat, drink some water, *something.* Just get away.

But guilt and self-disgust had eroded his appetite and he couldn't move away from his spot near the couch.

She stared at her laptop with dull eyes.

"Nyrene."

The only sign she'd even heard him was the flicker of her lashes.

"What's on the laptop?"

Finally, she rolled her head and stared at him. He almost wished she hadn't because, yet again, he could see the vicious, ugly bruising there. "My life," she said tonelessly.

He opened his mouth, but then she closed her eyes and settled deeper into the couch.

Setting his jaw, he grabbed the computer, prepared for

another attack.

Although her eyes opened, all she did was stare at him, defeat written all over her face.

He'd never thought he could be this disgusted with himself, but in the past two days, he'd surprised himself, and not in a good way.

Just destroy it. Once it's busted, nobody can track you.

He took it with him into the kitchen and put it down. It was an older model, clearly worn. He crouched in front of the sink, pulling out the toolbox under there. There was a hammer on top, just a plain claw hammer, but it would do the job.

As he stood, the little switch on the front caught his eye and he paused.

The Wi-Fi connection.

It was in the off position.

How...

With a curse, he tossed the hammer onto the counter and stood, hands braced in front of him as he fought to clear his head, do what he needed to do.

He knew all about that.

The Wi-Fi isn't on.

What did she mean anyway? *My life...*

He didn't know, couldn't understand what had driven her to move past the fear he kept seeing on her face every time she looked at him. That fear—*fuck*, what was he doing?

She was terrified of him and after last night—hell, after five minutes ago, she had more than enough reason, even if he hadn't dragged her up and down the mountains of Tennessee.

My life.

Shoving off the counter, he turned and stared at her.

She hadn't moved, not even an inch.

When he walked back across the floor and sat on the coffee table, she didn't blink.

He started, once more, going through her purse.

She hadn't called anybody. It wasn't possible. The phone hadn't even been *on*. Unless tracking had gotten a lot more complex, nobody could have located them using the phone.

He'd ditched his—*after* somebody had tried to ventilate his skull—but it still didn't explain how somebody had known he'd be there, at that truck stop, on that road.

And nothing explained how she'd *known*. Nobody could have contacted her unless it was done via skywriting and he would have probably noticed that.

But I already told you what was going on. You just didn't want to listen.

"Bullshit," he muttered, searching the purse itself now. Nothing in the lining that he could feel. Nothing, nothing, nothing...

I already told you.

He shoved upward and started to pace.

It was bullshit. Complete bullshit.

But...

Once you eliminate the impossible, whatever remains, no matter how improbable, must be the truth.

The quote leaped into his mind. He hadn't read Doyle in years, but he could see those words now, clear as day.

Whatever remains, no matter how improbable...

"Tell me about the truck stop."

There was no answer, but he made himself let it go. He'd pushed her too hard and she'd been through too much. He needed to think anyway.

"Here."

Nyrene opened her eyes and stared at the plate he'd just put on the coffee table, which was a plain, simple affair—nothing but a slab of wood and four legs. Pretty much everything in the cabin was plain and simple, including the bowl of pasta he'd put in front of her.

Her stomach revolted at the sight of it.

She just turned her face back into the couch.

"You need to eat."

"I can't eat that," she said softly. If he'd just shut up, she might sleep. Sleep would be welcome.

"Drink, then. You haven't had anything all afternoon."

She thought about telling him to fuck off, but didn't see the point. She eased her body around and reached for the glass he'd put by the plate, pausing when she saw the little white bottle. Ibuprofen.

"You should take some. It will help the swelling, maybe let you sleep a little better."

There was also an ice pack. She ignored that and

reached for the bottle, half-afraid to take anything from him. But the bottle was new, still sealed. She shook out four tablets and took them, washing them down with water that tasted metallic and flat. It was wet, though, and it cooled her abused throat. She had to fight the urge to puke it back up once it hit her stomach and the nervous knots it had twisted itself into, but she breathed through her nose and stared hard at the far wall until she was sure it would stay down.

She took another few sips, drinking roughly half of it before she eased back onto the couch.

"Tell me about the truck stop, Nyrene. What...how did you know they were there?"

There was an odd, grim note in his voice.

"Why? So you can yell at me again? I'm afraid I don't have much of anything else you can search, either." She opened her eyes to glare at him just as he shifted his attention toward her.

His gaze dipped and she tensed.

Ruddy, red color danced across his cheekbones before it faded. He opened his mouth, then closed it before shaking his head.

Hoping that was the end of it, she tucked herself into the corner, making her body as small as she could. The exhaustion dropped down onto her.

As she was drifting into sleep, she thought she felt somebody stroke her cheek, then something cool pressed against her face.

He ate mechanically, not tasting the canned pasta. It didn't do anything but fill the hole in his belly. Brooding, Dev focused on everything he'd found in her purse, looking for any one thing he could have missed, but there wasn't anything.

I don't have much of anything else you can search.

She'd had her fingers twisted in the neckline of her scrubs top, her knuckles bloodless from clutching so tightly. Scared, but that spark of temper showed.

As her breathing deepened, then slowed, he closed his eyes. He was exhausted himself and needed even just a few hours of sleep, but too many questions flooded his mind.

A shift of movement had him looking at her.

She'd fallen asleep.

He rose and carried his plate into the kitchen, along with hers. He'd eat it, too, although damn if he was hungry now. He didn't plan on leaving behind any sign that he'd been here, not even in the trash, so he'd eat the lousy food.

But first...

He moved back to the couch and crouched down, studying the bruising. It had deepened to a vicious purple now, her eye swollen, while the color spilled halfway down her cheek. He'd been terrified when he saw that son of a bitch drive his fist into her face, even more so when Morehead had picked her up.

His hands clenched involuntarily and he made himself relax. "Nyrene?"

She didn't stir.

Softly, he traced the bruise on her face. She flinched when he pressed down gently on the bones around her eye, but even that didn't wake her.

He didn't think anything had been broken, but she had to be hurting.

Frowning, he peeled the edge of her vee-neck top away. There was another bruise, starting at her shoulder. From being thrown against the seat belt when that drunk had rear-ended her. He'd been in a wreck or two himself. She probably felt like her entire body had been battered and what was he doing but adding to her discomfort?

He didn't know what to do about it, though.

She was tied into this and if he didn't keep her with him, she'd be grabbed. The thought flooded him with rage.

He twisted until he could pick up the icepack. It was already warming up, but it was better than nothing. The medical kit under the sink had a couple more and he'd take them along when they left. Carefully, he placed it against her cheek.

His fingers itched and he gave in to the urge to brush the soft, unmarked skin of her lower jaw. Then, because he had to say it, he murmured, "I'm sorry, Nyrene."

CHAPTER NINE

Nyrene woke to silence and pain.

She ached all over and her mind was muzzy.

She was also alone for the first time since she'd woken to find herself in the car with Bennett Deverall. Lying on her side, she studied the room through her lashes. There was no relief from the darkness in the cabin.

It was still dark outside. She didn't know how late, or early, it was, but the air had that odd, quiet feel that came in the hours just before dawn.

Easing her body up, she looked around, although she couldn't make out much of anything in the blackness.

He wasn't in there.

She didn't know how she knew, but she was positive he wasn't in there.

Slowly, she rose and made her way over to the window, looked out.

Her entire life had gone to shit in the past few days. The car wreck, the headaches, seeing him again in the ER and all those crazy, surreal images.

He's not to blame for that, Nye. Maybe everything seems to be tied to him, but his life is just as fucked up as yours.

Yeah.

She'd give him that.

But having *him* nearby seemed to be a health hazard, not to mention all the associated problems that were likely to come from this.

He'd stolen numerous cars—was she considered to be party to that? Was she looking at jail time?

I need to get away from him. Turn myself in. Her brain slid sideways at that thought, though, the idea of going to the cops in Clary flooding her with foreboding.

Then I won't go to Clary.

There were other cops. Other people she could talk to, weren't there? If there was corruption going on, there had to be somebody she could tell.

She didn't know. She couldn't figure it out here when she was constantly on edge and waiting to see who would be the next person to point a gun at him.

She fumbled around the room, searching for her things. She found her purse, but her computer wasn't in there. Her gut wrenched at the thought of leaving without it. She'd told Bennett her life was on that piece of equipment and she hadn't lied.

But she wouldn't die if she didn't have her computer. Most of what she had could be restored. She backed up most of her work so it was waiting for her...if she was able to get out of this mess.

I have to leave without it.

No, she wouldn't die without her computer, but she might die if she stayed here.

She did one more slow circuit around the room, wishing she'd taken the time to learn the layout of the place last night. Other than her, the cabin was empty and she had two choices...go out the front door or a window.

She chose a window, the one facing the back of the property, and she swallowed as she stared into the dark maw of endless night. Then, as carefully as she could, she lifted the blinds. The window resisted and she was sweating by the time she had it open. She gave one last look around and then slid outside.

The call of insects buzzing and the occasional night creature were the only sounds. She eased around the side of the small, square cabin, chancing a quick look at the front.

The truck he'd stolen was there.

She wished she had Bennett's handy knack for hotwiring, but she didn't. Wishes weren't going to get her out of there, either, so she moved away from the cover of the house, sticking to the tree line. She darted a look at the truck. He wasn't there. She shot a longer, harder look at the yard, such as it was, and he wasn't there, either.

Where was he?

It doesn't matter.

She hurried to the edge of the yard and started through the cover the trees offered. Every step she took sounded painfully loud and she ended up going at a snail's pace as she listened for any noise, searched for any movement that she might pick up in the darkness.

How long had they been on the pocked and pitted gravel road that had led them here? She didn't know. How long had she been walking? Eying the illuminated dial on her watch, she tried to figure it out. She had no idea.

She gave it ten more minutes and then she started to move faster. She had to get away—

An arm shot out and caught her, banded securely at her breasts, all but pinning her arms. A hand covered her mouth, stifling her scream.

Panicked, Nyrene drove her foot down and had the satisfaction of hearing a pained, masculine grunt as she connected with her attacker's foot. She tried to bite his hand, but his grip practically clamped her jaw shut.

When her feet left the ground, she struggled harder. Swiping her nails across the forearm holding her, she tried to draw blood. A voice rasped in her ear, but she couldn't understand it.

Get away!

Then, with a force that shocked her into silence, she was shoved up against a tree while a heavy male body pressed into hers. Some part of her recognized him even as he caught her wrists and pinned them overhead.

"Damn it, be *still*," Dev snarled. Fury and fear pulsed inside him.

She'd been quiet, so quiet he'd barely heard her as he did another patrol through the darkness. Two hours of sleep hadn't done much to take the edge off his exhaustion, but he'd gotten by on less, for longer, and he knew he couldn't afford not to stay on alert.

Nyrene still struggled, the movements frenzied, and he caught her chin, tried to force her head up so she could see him.

"It's *me*."

Her voice, when it came, was incredulous. "Is that

supposed to help me calm down, you son of a bitch?"

The comment threw him off guard, but only for a minute—what had he expected her to say? *Oh, hey...I was just out here looking for you?* Muffling a curse, he racked his brain, searching for something, *anything* he could say that would ease the tension in her body, the fear that all but bled from her.

"What are you doing?" he asked softly.

Nyrene was so taut, he thought she might snap. The silence hummed between them and then finally, she said, "I wanted to get *out* of here. Is that so hard to get? I'm *terrified.* You've got people shooting at you. Ever since *you* showed up in my life, everything around me has gone crazy...including *me*. You scared me to death when you showed up at my house. You think I'm involved with...hell, I don't *know* you, but unless my book club or my critique group is more dangerous than I thought, then you are barking up the wrong tree. You're stealing cars and...and..."

She stuttered to a stop and he heard her swallow.

Weary, he said, "I don't want to hurt you. I don't want to...." Absently, he rubbed his thumb against the soft skin of one of her wrists. "*Have* I hurt you?"

She didn't answer and then she jerked her wrists. "*This* doesn't exactly feel *good.*"

He was a monstrous son of a bitch because his immediate response was...*Yes, it does.*

She felt good. The lush curves of her body pillowing his, the scent of her hair and skin—honeysuckle and oranges—flooding his head. He could feel his body responding.

He eased back, shifting his lower body away. "I'm going to let you go, but don't take off. Please don't make me have to run you down."

With a soft, broken sigh, she slumped. He couldn't make out much of anything in the nonexistent light, save for the shape of her face, the curve of her cheek, but he didn't have to see her to know he'd put that dread back in her eyes.

"Why are you doing this?" she whispered. "Why can't you just let me go?"

Because you're in as much danger as I am now. "Come on," he said tersely. "We need to get inside."

When she didn't immediately move, Dev clenched his

jaw. If she fought, he'd have to scare her. Again. But she moved away from the tree. He could make out her form, just barely, and the slumped set of her shoulders, how she moved with her head bowed. It made him that much more disgusted with himself.

"Look," he said, keeping his voice low. He faltered for the words, but they never came. "Never mind."

They walked. She'd gone maybe an eighth of a mile— not very far, but in the dark, unfamiliar surroundings, she'd moved quickly enough. But, once out of the trees, walking on the sad excuse of a road, they moved much quicker.

They were almost to the clearing where the cabin sat when he froze.

A low noise came to him in the night. The faint hum of a motor on the road, probably almost half a mile away. The only reason he even pegged it as *wrong* was because he'd spent too many nights out here and he knew every sound—the way the wind could whisper or moan through the trees, and the music of the surrounding wildlife.

As he stood there, it grew faintly louder.

"In the trees," he said, forcing the words out. *"Now."*

"But..."

"Do it!" He caught her arm with his left hand, drawing the Glock M17 from his holster with his right. They moved into the trees, deeper and deeper until he trusted the cover. He could still see the gravel road. Just barely, but it was enough. With one eye on her and the other on the road, he waited.

"What are—"

"Quiet!"

Not even thirty seconds later, he heard her startled inhalation of breath.

She'd heard it now, too.

"This is why I wanted to leave," she muttered. "I *knew* something was wrong. You're going to get me killed."

"No." He hoped he wasn't lying. "Now shut up."

The car stopped before it reached the clearing and that filled Dev with more trepidation. He hadn't heard them leave the car, but they had—he just knew it. *Fuck*, they were quiet. Leaning in, he pressed his mouth to her ear. "Don't make a sound, Nyrene. And don't *move*."

Her only response was a single jerk of her head. It

would have to be enough. He needed his hands free. Carefully, he eased away, ears straining as he listened to the night. The insects had gone quiet and the low murmur of the other night creatures had ceased.

They were on their way in.

He eased one foot forward, checking the ground before he shifted his weight, then another. His goal was the big cypress that lay between him and the road. He had just barely reached it when he saw them. One of them had a penlight out, just a thin sliver of illumination sweeping the ground.

He counted three, watched as they passed, and listened.

Nothing. But his gut told him that was all. He inched away from the tree. It seemed it took hours to cross a single foot and he was soaked with sweat, his muscles locked by the time he had reached the edge of the trees. There was probably a good ten yards between him and Nyrene, and barely twenty between him and the men who had crouched behind his truck.

He held his Glock in a two-handed grip, watching as they fanned out. One went left. One went right. The other crept up the stairs.

The low, frenzied curse came before he expected it.

One of the men came running out from behind the house. "She's not here." It was grimly delivered, the words soft, just barely loud enough to carry to where Dev waited in the trees.

Fury gnawed at him. They were looking for Nyrene. She'd lied to him.

"What do you want to do?"

It was the same speaker.

He hadn't moved an inch.

Somebody else had, though. Dev felt somebody approaching as clearly as if the bastard had tugged some invisible wire.

"Man, she ain't here. The truck's cold. They probably ditched it here and moved. Somehow, she's staying ahead—"

"Silence!" The word came out too close to Dev and it came in a low, controlled order. Not good...

Dev forced himself to relax and then he moved out from behind the tree. His target was the shadow that was darker than the other. He aimed at the chest and pulled the trigger.

He dove into a crouch, moving before he even waited to see if his target had gone down.

"Shit!" It came in a low, sharp hiss and Dev eased out from behind the tree, peering into the night.

There was another shadow now, closer, coming toward him at a sharp angle, but this one's movements were slower, less certain. The man didn't even pause by the body, just kept moving.

Dev took aim, squeezed.

The man moved at the exact same time.

Baring his teeth, Dev went to move.

And couldn't.

Something flung him up against the tree while a vise closed around his neck. He swung upward and encountered *nothing*.

"Where is the girl?"

The pressure on his throat eased. Dev's mind whirled to process what was happening.

Nobody was *touching* him. No *thing* was touching him.

"Don't make me ask again," the man said, moving closer. The pressure around Dev's throat intensified, as if in warning, and then it relaxed, yet again.

"Fuck..." Dev managed to get that much out before he was slammed back up against the tree.

A sharp, shrill scream filled the night air. For one moment, he had control of his body again and he jerked up the Glock as the second man rushed into the trees. He squeezed and felt the wet of blood gush over him as his attacker fell into him. Out of reaction, Dev caught the body and used it as a shield, backing away.

"Pete!"

It was the talker again.

"*Pete*! Where are you?"

Dev didn't know if he should be grateful for the man's idiocy or annoyed. The man stumbled right past him and Dev eased the body he held—Pete, he guessed—to the ground and then straightened. Faint, watery light was starting to filter in through the trees, the first glimpse of dawn.

It wasn't a lot of light, but Dev didn't need much.

He aimed—and this time, a scream filled the air as the man went down, blood gushing from his leg.

Dev strode toward him.

"Don't touch him!"

Nyrene's panicked shout was filled with rage and other emotions he couldn't decipher. When she came stumbling out of the dark, he caught her. "That son of a bitch is here to kill me. But sure, why not? I won't touch him." He stormed forward, his hands already itching.

"Don't!" Nyrene shoved in between them. "Don't," she said again, her voice panting. "He's not here for you."

"Yeah. I got that memo." Dev shoved past her and bent down, flipping the injured man over onto his stomach, ignoring the scream of pain. Pulling his cuffs from his belt, he slapped one on the man's wrist. "He's here for you. Don't know where they're taking you or who sent them but maybe it's time—"

His fingers caught the man's other wrist. Cold.

His skin was—

"Help me roll over," the man said, his voice calm.

"Yeah," Dev said. He did just that—still touching the man's wrist. He didn't even blink when the man moved, swift and smooth, and then their positions were reversed. His wrist was held. The icy cold grip of the man's hand was bone jarring, enough to make his teeth ache. But he couldn't pull away.

"Give me your gun, pal."

Dev looked down, stared at the Glock M17 he still held. "Give you the—"

"*No!*"

No. Yeah, that sounded good. Did he want to turn over his weapon? That didn't seem right.

"Come on. Turn it over."

He lifted his hand.

Something hit him.

Blinking, he found himself lying flat on his back and staring up at the sky. Blood roared in his ears. His arm ached from the cold, and in the next moment his mind cleared. Sharpened.

"What the—"

"Get up." Nyrene's voice was thin and shaky.

He jerked upright.

"That..." Dev shook his head. "That... What the—"

Nyrene's gaze jumped to his. "I don't know what."

He looked at the Glock, at the man who was now trying to inch back. He took the weapon and leveled it.

Maybe I am going crazy.

Nyrene slicked her damp hands down the sides of her scrub pants. The scrubs were wrinkled, and now that they were in the cabin, she could see how filthy they'd gotten during her aborted escape.

Her heart slammed hard against her ribs and it had nothing to do with the fact that Dev was busy tying an injured man to a chair. No, her heart was slamming because of what she'd seen playing out in her head.

In her *head*, she'd watched as Dev turned over his gun.

The man had told him to turn around and when Dev asked why, the man had laughed. So I can shoot you in the back of the head. I do that, then leave the gun with Pete— he's the one they'll pin your murder on. I don't need cops chasing me.

Then she'd seen Dev actually lift his hand to *give* the son of a bitch his weapon.

"This isn't happening." She rubbed her hands up and down her face. "This isn't happening."

"Yeah. Keep saying that," Bennett said, his voice hard. "Let me know if it works."

She swallowed as he crouched in front of the stranger. "You..." Bennett said, hitting him on the knee. "I'm going to ask you some questions. Every time you lie—"

"What?" The man sneered. "You'll shoot me?"

"You only wish."

She sucked in a shocked breath as Bennett struck, driving a fist into the man's gut. He crumpled and Bennett moved back.

Both of them stared at Bennett with a mix of curiosity and fear as he grabbed something from his boot. She saw the flash of light off metal.

"You ain't..." Now the man's voice wobbled. "You ain't going to use that."

"Yeah. I am."

Nyrene saw blood.

She was a nurse. Blood didn't bother her. Puke didn't bother her. Plenty of disgusting things didn't affect her, but the sight of the blood streaming down the man's cheek made her start to shake.

"Now...you're going to talk." Bennett flipped a chair around and straddled it, rocking forward to stare at the bound man. "Start with your name, then tell me what's going on—why you're here, how you found us, why you want Nyrene. All of it."

CHAPTER TEN

"Car four."

Dev looked at the soft-spoken woman as she settled on the rich leather of the Escalade. It was black, expensive and smelled faintly of pipe smoke.

"Four times a charm," he said, his voice flat. He figured he might as well make use of it since the men who'd come after them no longer needed it. Only one of them was still alive, and he was cuffed. He had one hand free and could get to the food Dev had left out. He wouldn't starve.

Dev would let somebody know where he was, sooner or later.

But he had other problems.

Namely, the woman sitting next to him.

When she told you she saw *it, she meant...she saw it. The bitch is psychic, man!* Those words had all but been screeched out after the man Dev had found in the woods realized his options—talk or hurt. He'd talked. A lot.

Okay. Psychic.

That meant...

His gut churned.

"I'm sorry."

All Nyrene did was sink deeper into the seat, clutching her purse awkwardly. He'd returned her laptop. Despite what rational thought was telling him, Dev knew the son of a bitch back at the cabin hadn't been lying. Somehow, Nyrene had people tracking her.

They didn't have to see her, tag her with a tracking device or anything.

They were tracking her because she was *psychic*.

That meant when she'd kept him out of the garage it was because she was trying to help.

That meant when she'd told him not to go home, she'd saved his life.

And...*fuck*, it wasn't the first time. She'd told him she'd gone to the hospital after she'd seen him on the news, or rather, seen the news of his death.

Every single time he'd put fear in her eyes, it had filled him with disgust and the weight of it now was magnified tenfold. He could feel the guilt like chains around him, dragging him down.

"Nyrene—"

"Don't." She pulled her knees to her chest and hid her face against them. "Just...don't, okay? What does it matter anyway? I was pretty much fucked the minute I saw you in the ER."

"I'm..." He swore. Throwing the Escalade into drive, he did a rough, three-point turn on the narrow road. "You should have just stayed away."

"I couldn't." Her voice was muffled. "And it's done. So just don't."

"I'll get you out of this."

"Yeah." She laughed tiredly. "Sure you will."

He wanted to tell her to trust him. Which was a joke. According to everything he'd heard in the past hour, and everything he'd seen her do over the past two days, he was the only reason she was in trouble to begin with.

"Get some sleep," he said as he pulled out onto the road. The sun was finally coming up over the horizon, burning away the fog.

"How am I supposed to sleep now?"

The question was softly spoken and he doubted she expected an answer. He gave her one, though.

"You're safe right now."

I'll do my damnedest to make sure you stay that way, too.

* * * * *

"She hasn't disappeared off the face of the earth." Taige listened to Joss on the other end of the line for another minute and then she interrupted, "Look, big guy. I know what I saw. I've been living with this shit in my head a long time—"

She hissed out a breath and held the phone a few inches away from her ear. "Fine. Fine. *Fine.* You gave her the card, right? Okay then. You did what you could. Now we wait."

She hung up the phone in the middle of his rant.

He wasn't mad at her.

Taige hadn't worked with Joss Crawford in a good long while, but she had worked with him before. His mood was foul, but it was more about the situation than anything else.

She could understand.

Dirty cops were a bitch to deal with. Joss wasn't only trying to make sure the girl stayed alive, he had to keep her away from a mess of dirty cops.

She had her own mess to deal with, though.

"I'll tell you what," she muttered, rubbing her brow as she tried to make sense of the report her assistant had given her. "I'll trade you places. You come play boss man out here and I'll go hunt down your new psychic."

"Talking to yourself already?"

The voice was enough to make her smile. She glanced up as her husband came through the door. Cullen Morgan was, and always had been, enough to make her heart stutter. "Trying to make sense out of all of this—make my way through this and figure out the cases we *need* to take, which ones we *should* take, which ones I should pass along to Jones." She sighed and pushed back from the desk.

A few months earlier, Elise Oswald, the woman who'd headed up the Oswald Group, had died. It had been sudden and brutal and had caught everybody by surprise.

Everybody but Oz, it seemed.

She'd left her company, lock, stock and barrel, to Taige.

Taige barely knew Oz, but the letter she'd been given during the reading of the will had spelled out some things very clearly. Though she hadn't known Oz well, Oz had known her. Or known about her. And she'd decided Taige was the only person she could trust to head up her security company.

"I'm not equipped for this," she said softly as Cullen

came around to kiss her temple. "I don't do *reports*. I don't handle *finances*. I don't do *payroll*, for fuck's sake."

"To be fair, that's hired out." As he straightened, he rested a hand on the back of her neck and dug his fingers into muscles gone tight. "And you're handling things. It's just the administrative work that's driving you crazy."

"Crazy?" She laughed weakly. "It's giving me a migraine and making me want to rip out my hair. Cullen...I'm out of my league here. Yeah, I can handle delegating, and I can handle figuring out which of Oz's people are ideal for a certain job, but the rest of it? I am *lost,* but it's not like I can just throw an ad in the paper— Needed: office manager for psychic security group."

"True."

She rested her head against the back of the chair and looked up at him.

His eyes were calm. "You'll figure it out, baby."

"Yeah. I hope so. But first I've got to get a handle on what's going on with this woman I had to tell Jones about. My brain isn't letting it go." She rested her hand on his chest as he bent to kiss her.

"You need to clear your head for a bit."

"Yeah." Swiveling the chair around, she stared up at her husband. "You maybe wanna take me out to lunch? Help me clear *your* head?"

"I can help you with that." He lowered his mouth to her neck and scraped the arch of it with his teeth. "How hungry are you?"

As he came around to stand in front of her, Taige slid him a smile. "Actually, not that hungry at all. Got something else in mind?"

Oman stared at the bloody body of his ex-partner.

While Morehead hadn't realized it until it was too late, he'd just been fired—in the most extreme way possible.

Oman hadn't done the deed, although he wished he could have.

Too easy to track back to him. He wasn't a cop for nothing. There was no *perfect* crime.

No, he'd just arranged for Morehead to cross paths with some men who had serious issues with the young, arrogant shithead. The boss hadn't been pleased. It would have been better if Morehead had just fallen in line, the way he was supposed to, but Oman had seen this coming.

He'd been preparing for this very eventuality.

"We're going to find the son of a bitch who did this, Oman."

Oman looked up as the investigating officer came around to stop at his side.

"Yeah." He nodded and kept the mask of fury in place as he looked away from the dead man.

"This place is going to shit." Dugan pulled a pack of cigarettes from his jacket and shook one out. He offered one to Oman, but tucked the pack away after the other cop shook his head. "First all, this bullshit with Deverall. I'm not buying it. I'm just not. And now..."

The hands Oman had shoved into his pockets curled into fists. Deverall. What he'd *wanted* to do was find some way to implicate *him*. If he could paint the bastard as a cop killer, then he'd have less to worry about, but nobody who knew the man was going to buy him going crazy like that. He was about as straight as they came, and too fucking smart.

"Yeah," Oman said as Dugan went quiet. Then he looked around. "Is there anything I can do around here? Help in any way?"

"No." Dugan shook his head. "Nah, you just go home. Have a drink. When you can, I need the names of people you think could have done this. We'll have to go through your case files, but maybe you can help narrow the field. But for now, turn your head off."

With a strained smile, Oman nodded and walked away, careful to keep his body language on point. Shoulders slumped, head bowed. From under his lashes, he looked around, watching the scurry of the techs gathering evidence, watching the faces of the officers who'd responded to the call.

It hadn't taken them long to find the dead cop, but the body hadn't been hidden, either.

That was for the best. If another cop went missing, people would be looking hard at the department, probably already were, but they'd tag this as a vengeance killing, which it was. *Missing* made for a lot more questions, sometimes, than *dead*.

"You're smooth."

The voice came out of the shadows near Oman's car.

Oman drew his weapon. The gun fit easily, comfortably, into his big hands. Eyes scanning the darkness, he took a few steps to the right. The big van parked there blocked the light spilling out onto the street and highlighting his ass, making him a big, easy target.

Before he could say anything, a woman moved out the shadows. She lifted a brow at him. "Don't worry. I'm not here to cause you any problems. I'm actually here to *help*."

"I'm good, thanks."

Her gaze bored into his. Oman didn't like this—her, the look on her face or the way her mouth slowly curved into a smile.

"You're good," she agreed after a moment. "But you're not going to get to him before he gets the word out about you. Not unless you have some help."

Oman didn't blink. He'd always been told his poker face was excellent. But he couldn't do a damn thing about the cold line of sweat that began to drip down his back. Couldn't silence the sudden rush of fear that gripped him and twisted savagely. Still, he managed to smile pleasantly. "I'm afraid I don't know what you're talking about."

Her heels clicked on the pavement as she moved closer. "You sure that's the line you want to go with, Lieutenant Oman? Or would you rather the two of us sit down and talk about just how I can help you get your hands on Bennett Deverall?"

The sunlight was hard, hot, and bright, bouncing off the river to blind him as he waited for her to speak.

They'd moved someplace a little more private.

Oman still didn't know her name.

He very much wanted to know her name, and who'd hired her, but he wasn't stupid. This wasn't the time or the place.

"So." She smiled at him as she sipped from a bottle of water. "You know what I need now. I know what you need, *and* I can help you get it. It's an arrangement that will benefit you, me...and your boss. I imagine he's getting rather tired of being disappointed."

"If you have information on Officer Deverall, you could have just called the tip line." He gave her a charming smile.

"Hmmm. But then I don't get what I need. And you don't want him going in to give a statement, answer questions about his house. It was clever, though, how you set it up. Fuck up the gas, let it fill his house. Not to mention how your men handled it all. Did you know he had some issues with the wiring in the house or did they figure it out while they were there?"

With every word, his heart beat faster. With every word, he could feel the tremor in his hands worsen.

"No answer?" She shrugged. "That's okay. It doesn't matter. I was just admiring your clever handling of the matter. It would have worked, too. Too bad he had a warning."

He smiled and leaned in. The water she still held splashed the front of his shirt as he all but crushed it between them. Her eyes were wide, studying his face.

He took his gun and pressed it into her abdomen, just off to the side.

And she still *smiled*.

"That's a gun, cupcake," he said. "It's not anything I'd be smiling about if I were you."

"Oh, come on now." She cocked her head, the sweep of her short red hair brushing the collar of her shirt. "You don't want to shoot me. Well, okay, you do. But you won't—not here—and if you'd just listen, I'll tell you things that will make you *very* glad you didn't shoot me."

"Like what?" he growled, pressing the muzzle deeper.

Pain flickered in her eyes and her mouth tightened. But that easy calm didn't leave her face. "Like where you can find Deverall...tonight. I can tell you that. Do whatever you want with him once you find him. Just make sure I get the woman he has with him."

* * * * *

The motel room was bland and boring.

It was also clean, which was more than Nyrene could say about herself.

A bag of clothes was on the bed and as soon as she had the okay, she was disappearing into the bathroom and parking her dirty, tired self in there for a month or more.

Her cop turned kidnapper turned wannabe protector was outside. She wasn't going to make a break for it. Even if he hadn't just gone to grab some drinks from vending, even if he'd decided to hit the strip club two lots down, she still wouldn't have left. She would probably be sitting next to him as he tucked bills into some lithe, pretty thing's G-string.

They'd been looking for *her*.

Those guys who'd been at the truck stop and shot at them hadn't been looking for him. They were looking for her.

The door opened and she jolted, coming off the bed with her heart racing and her hands clenched.

The adrenaline drained away as she met Bennett's eyes.

"I thought you'd be in the shower." He glanced at the bag from the discount department store. "Is something wrong?"

"No." She licked her lips and reached for the bag. Nerves made her awkward and she picked it up without moving her purse. The bright pink bag upended and the contents went everywhere. Swearing, she tossed the bag down and started picking up all the junk she hauled around.

Keys, two—no, *three*—packs of gum, all half-gone, tampons and pens and loose change. Enough loose change to keep them in vending machine soft drinks for a week, it seemed.

"Here."

She looked up as Bennett held out her wallet.

"Thanks." She gingerly accepted it, careful not to let her fingers touch him.

He noticed.

The stilted silence settled around them, heavy and thick.

She hated it, right up until he asked, "That's what causes it, isn't it? Touching somebody?"

The strength drained out of her and she sat down hard on her ass, her tablet in one hand, a tampon in the other. Looking down at her hands, she blushed and shoved both items into her purse. "I don't know," she said quietly. "When people were touching me in the ER, trying to get me to calm down, that made it *worse* but it was like I could hear them, screaming inside my head. Nothing's connected to them, though. Right now, it's all..."

She stopped speaking, uncertain how to even finish.

"Me." He looked as tired as she felt, and she watched as he sat down as well, his back against the bed.

He still wore the hoodie but it was unzipped and she could see the butt of his gun. She'd seen him use it, or close enough. She'd caught a glimpse of his body, hidden by the darkness, as he'd used that weapon on the men who'd come looking for her.

Unaware of her thoughts, he said tiredly, "This is all about me. You wouldn't be in this mess if it wasn't for me."

"No." She squirmed as he looked at her from the corner of his eye. "I could very well be in the psych ward for a twenty-three-hour hold."

"Twenty-three hours came and went, Nyrene."

Yeah. It was all a blur, too. As the man next to her sighed, she went back to collecting the rest of the change. "Bennett?"

He looked at her through his lashes.

"I know you didn't...well, I know this wasn't anything you intended to happen."

His lids flickered. Shaking his head, he said, "The road to hell is paved with good intentions—isn't that the saying? It's just...everything you said sounded..."

"Impossible," she offered when he lapsed into silence.

"Yeah." He snorted. "Turns out it was just highly improbable."

Nyrene didn't entirely understand the look in his eyes, but she had a good idea what was behind it. He felt guilty—yeah, he *should*—and he was sorry, which he'd already admitted. She had to be honest, though. Had somebody told her this, or anything like it, would happen to her, she would have laughed her butt off.

Crazy things just didn't happen to Nyrene Goldman. She had a nice, normal life, and she *liked* it that way.

She rose and settled her purse on the bed—in the middle.

"Here."

She glanced at him and saw the card he was holding out.

As she reached for it, he said, "You've got more stuff in that purse than I would have thought was possible."

"Yeah." She glanced at the card and went to tuck it into her bag, but then, before she did, she stopped.

Slowly, she held it up.

"Shit."

She dropped down on the edge of the bed, staring dumbly at the card. Where had this...?

No. Wait. She remembered.

That guy—the one in the doctor's office. Big and rough and built. He'd handed her a card, as though she'd dropped it. But she hadn't.

He must have given it to her.

She couldn't think of any other way she'd be holding a card with FBI printed on it. There was also a name. She closed her eyes while the name echoed in her mind.

Taige Morgan.

She sucked in a breath.

"What—"

She didn't hear him, barely noticed as he gently tugged the card away.

Taige Morgan—if there was anybody in the southern states who *hadn't* heard of her, Nyrene would be shocked.

But how did she know about Nyrene?

Call me.

Bennett stared at the words scrawled below the name—and that name was a sucker punch. *Taige Morgan.*

"This shit is just getting crazier," he muttered.

The bed squeaked and he looked up, watched as Nyrene collected the bag.

"What are you doing?"

"Taking a shower," she replied and her voice wobbled.

It all but broke him as she cleared her throat and then continued, although he could see how shaken she was. "I need a shower. That's a nice, normal thing, right? I need nice and normal."

"Okay." He nodded and closed his fingers around the card. "Okay."

He watched as she disappeared into the bathroom and then he blew out a harsh breath. This was...

Hell. He didn't know what to even *call* the situation they'd wound up in. FUBAR just might cover it, but he wasn't sure. And he'd dragged an innocent woman into it.

He'd scared her half to death, and more than once, he'd put her life at risk.

As the water in the bathroom came on, he closed his eyes.

Immediately, he opened them. Tossing the card down, he shoved upright and started to pace. His imagination served up a detailed image of just what was happening in the small bathroom. The water raining down on her, sluicing over all that lovely, golden skin, to her breasts and then her belly...

Fuck.

He stopped at the door and leaned forward, hands braced on it while his body raged and burned. *Stop it, man. You gotta stop it.*

He drew in a slow breath, held it a moment then blew it out. Then he repeated the process a few more times, lying to himself all the while that he had it under control.

He didn't believe the lie, but he believed he could fake it.

He could—

A short, sharp scream sliced through the air.

He drew his Glock and shouted, "Nyrene!"

There wasn't an answer.

Shit.

The door was locked.

He reared back and busted through.

And then he had to jerk back to keep from stumbling over her. She was sitting on the tile, a towel wrapped around her. And everything that had been on the counter—ice bucket, the toothbrushes he'd grabbed, a couple bottles of water—was scattered all over the floor.

A soft, shaky gasp fell from her lips and he crouched down in front of her, almost afraid to touch her.

"Nyrene, are you hurt?" He holstered his weapon.

She lifted her head and looked at him. Her black hair hung in thick, wet ropes, clinging to her neck and shoulders. Water still beaded on her forehead, and as he watched, one drop slid down her temple and followed the elegant line of her cheek.

"What's wrong, baby?" The endearment slipped free before he realized it.

He didn't think she even noticed. Her eyes came to his, dark and haunted. She looked at him for just a blink and then averted her gaze. "I'm just...it's stupid. I'm okay."

"What's wrong?"

Now he did touch her, pushing her wet hair back from her face before he caught her chin and guided her gaze back to his. "Tell me."

"It's *stupid,*" she said. Her voice cracked and tears rolled out of her eyes. "I don't have any lotion and I don't have the conditioner for my hair and I don't have—"

A hard shudder racked her body and she clamped her lips tightly. After a few seconds, she said again, "It's stupid."

Dev wasn't so sure he agreed. He'd found her in the parking lot while a couple of assholes were trying to kidnap her. He had a good idea of what they would have done to her, too. He'd dragged her halfway across the state, interrogating her, and when she'd told him the truth, he hadn't believed her.

Now she was in a small, tired old motel with him and she didn't have anything but the clothes he'd grabbed for her from a local Walmart.

"Come on."

He held out a hand and waited until she placed hers in his. With her other, she clutched the towel between her breasts, holding it in place. He let go of her hand once she stood in front of the mirror.

He took another towel from the rod and started to dry her hair.

She didn't move or speak.

Taking the comb, he went to work on the tangles in her heavy hair, focusing on that task, and that alone. His entire body ached and he wanted to crowd up against her, press his mouth to her neck as he tugged the towel away she held so tightly.

But he just combed her hair.

Once it lay smooth against her back, he put the comb down. There were things he needed to say, things he *should* say, but when she turned around to look at him, his mind went blank.

He was still struggling to think past the hazy heat when she slid past him and into the bedroom.

He followed her.

"Am I ever going to be able to go back home?" she asked quietly.

Dev didn't know how to answer that—lying to her

wouldn't help and neither would the truth. *I don't know.*

Her breath hitched in her throat and she averted her face, staring at the far wall as she struggled not to cry.

One tear slid free.

"Hey..." He brushed it away and a harsh sob tore out of her.

Because he didn't know what else to do, Dev wrapped his arms around her as she started to cry.

CHAPTER ELEVEN

Her head ached.

Her throat felt raw.

And under her cheek, she felt the steady, strong beat of Dev's heart.

She didn't remember how she'd gotten here. She barely remembered anything after she'd climbed out of the shower, frustrated with the tangles in her hair and even more frustrated with the itchy feel of her skin, caused by the motel's cheap soap.

She knew she'd started to cry.

She knew that he'd brushed out the tangles in her hair.

She knew he'd held her.

And now she knew, intimately, how that big, long body of his felt pressed up against hers.

But she had no idea how long she'd cried, why she'd started, when he'd picked her up or lain down on the bed with her. Her brain was just a muzzy mess.

She had no desire to move, either.

His breath was a warm caress on her face and neck.

His body was incredibly strong under hers, and as she pondered that—the heavy, hard strength of him—she became aware of something else that was heavy and hard.

His cock was pressed up against her hip.

He'd tugged the edge of the sheet over them, tucking it around her body so she wasn't lying there in just a towel that barely covered her.

The sheet was miserable protection.

The towel was miserable protection.

Even his jeans didn't provide much of a barrier.

She felt him pulse against her and she flexed her hand

before tightening it into the material of his shirt. An answering pang echoed out from her core and blood rushed to her face.

Maybe it was the adrenaline thing—she could very well be running for her life—but Nyrene's mind started to rush and race with images of the two of them stretched out over the bed, his body crushing into hers as he moved back and forth between her thighs.

This man had terrified her.

This man had all but called her a liar.

And he'd rushed into the bathroom when she'd sent everything flying to the floor, his weapon in hand, his eyes fierce.

Instead of telling her to get over all the things she might well have to leave behind, he'd tended to her with gentle hands, drying her hair and combing away the tangles.

Now he held her.

It was *insane* to want him. Insane...and she knew it.

But she didn't care.

She'd tried to be careful her *entire* life.

She had gone to school and become a nurse. Her parents had said it was a nice, secure job.

She had bought a boring car and always drove the speed limit.

She'd dated the right kind of guy—an accountant who drove the speed limit and had regular dental check-ups and tipped exactly seventeen percent, regardless of the service, good or bad.

Her life had been normal and predictable. Then she discovered her boyfriend wasn't the good, stand-up guy she'd believed, but a *married* bastard with kids in multiple states.

She'd had somebody slam into her as she drove home. She'd willed herself not to cry until she was inside her house.

Then the headaches, the... *visions*, and Dev.

She'd tried to be good her whole life and now she was in a motel with a man who made her burn, and in the back of her mind lurked a knowledge. *You can't go home if you end up dead, Nye.*

Slowly, she lifted her head. The strong line of his neck was in front of her, not even an inch from her mouth.

Opening her hand, she kept her palm flat against his skin while his heart banged harder and faster.

She'd never taken chances. Fear kept her from going after the *one* thing she'd always wanted and now she was running for her life.

She didn't even think it through. She just closed the distance between them and pressed her mouth to his neck.

Dev stopped breathing.

At least it felt that way.

His body went to stone as she rubbed her lips over his skin.

She went to kiss him again and he shifted, spilling her onto her back so that she lay in the middle of the bed.

He was off the mattress and pacing, the next second.

His gaze came to hers. Self-conscious, she licked her lips, but she didn't look away.

His lids drooped and her heart skipped a beat as she realized he was staring at her mouth.

"Dev..."

He shook his head like a man coming out of a spell, and then he turned away.

"The card—you saw what it said. Do we need to leave here now or can you get some rest?" he asked, his voice lower, rougher.

"I don't want to sleep."

He jerked his head in a nod. "Okay. I need to shower and then—"

She let the towel fall away as she stood.

Dev's eyes slid down, down, down. It was like a caress and she was torn between grabbing the towel or grabbing *him*.

"I don't want to sleep," she said again. She took one step toward him and when he just continued to stare, she took another. "You want me...don't you?"

One long stride closed the distance between them and he reached up, gripping her shoulders in hard hands. "I don't think *want* covers it. But this... You're not thinking..."

"If you tell me I'm not thinking clearly, I'll hit you," she warned. She hadn't ever hit anybody, but she thought she just might enjoy hitting him if he said those words. Narrowing her eyes, she said, "I'm thinking just *fine*. I'm thinking about the fact that a couple of days ago, I drove by my boyfriend's office only to discover it wasn't *his* office and when I called, I got his *wife* on the phone, then I found out he's got kids in two different states. I'm thinking about how my head feels like it's going to come apart and I'm thinking about all the shit I'm seeing, the voices that won't shut up and all the stuff I see happening—something that my *head* tells me is impossible, but I see it anyway. And..."

She sucked in a breath as her words tumbled to a stop.

His thumb stroked over her skin and she shivered. "I'm thinking that for all I know, I'll be dead in a week, in two days, in two *hours* even. And I don't want the *emptiness* that's been my life for the past couple of years to be the *only* thing I can look back on."

She waited for him to break away.

She waited for him to say something sensible and logical in his low, harsh voice.

And while she was waiting, he backed her up against the narrow table tucked in next to the wall. "So what do you want?"

His thumb did another slow stroke against the sensitive skin of her upper chest.

"I want you."

His thigh pushed between hers as he crowded in closer. He lowered his head and pressed a kiss to the spot just below her ear. "If I was any kind of decent—"

"I don't want decent."

His kiss stole the breath out of her lungs. She shivered and pressed closer as he skimmed one hand up her back and fisted it in her hair. Then, as he caught her tongue and sucked it into his mouth, he tugged her head back.

She pressed closer, tangling her fingers in his shirt as he started to stab his tongue into her mouth. She felt that rhythmic pang between her thighs again—felt the hot, wet rush as her body prepared for him.

Mindless, she slid a hand down his chest, but then he caught her wrist.

Dev panted as he stared down at her. "I don't have any condoms."

"I'm clean." She blushed as she said it, but she kept her eyes on his. "The son of a bitch I was dating— I...I wasn't ready to sleep with him and that's why he was making time with another woman. But I haven't been with anybody since my senior year in college and I've had blood work done."

"That...none of that matters. We shouldn't—"

"Are *you* clean?"

His hand tightened on her hip. "Yeah, but you shouldn't believe me. You're a fucking nurse, Nyrene."

"Yeah. That means I'm aware of how stupid this is...and I *still don't care.*" She leaned forward, straining against the hold he had on her hair. He relaxed his grip and she rose onto her toes, sinking her teeth into his lower lip.

He groaned and cupped the back of her head, but she averted her face and pushed against his chest. "I'm on the pill. It's just...easier. Assuming I *live* through this, there's nothing else to worry about—and don't tell me not to believe you. You wouldn't even lie to me when I asked if I'd ever be able to go home and that was a much simpler lie than this would be."

His hand slid up and cupped her breast. She held her breath as he did it, and she tensed, waiting for him to squeeze too hard or pinch too tightly. Instead, he stroked his thumb along the sensitive skin under her areola, slowly working higher until he could circle his way around her nipple.

"Are you sure?" he whispered, pressing his mouth to her ear.

"Yes."

The room whirled as he caught her around the waist with his arm and lifted her.

His mouth took hers again, rough and demanding.

*Bed...*she thought blearily.

But instead of the bed, she felt the cool, hard surface of the wall and she arched closer, rubbing against the heavy length of him.

A guttural noise escaped Dev as he kissed his way down her neck, pausing to rub his lips along the line where the seat belt had marked her.

She whimpered when he closed his mouth around her nipple. His mouth was a sin—hot and sure, his teeth scraping against her flesh in the sweetest possible way.

One hand smoothed up her thigh, caught her hip and pulled her in closer. She gasped at the contact and then, with a desperation that might have shamed her had she been able to think, she said, "Please... I need to feel you inside me."

His entire body shuddered.

And in the next moment, he eased back, studying her face.

Her legs wobbled when he relaxed his hold around her waist, and then they all but melted as he reached for the button on his jeans, then the zipper, staring at her the entire time.

Dazed, she watched him free his cock, giving it one careless stroke. His blue eyes burned into hers and the heat of his body left her feeling scorched.

"Um..." her voice cracked. "The bed?"

"Fuck the bed." He boosted her up and she automatically curled her legs around his hips.

The first brush of his cock against her had her tensing.

"Nyrene?"

"Please..."

Dev would kick his own ass for this.

Later.

The hot, wet kiss of her pussy against the head of his cock had rational thought floundering to a halt. He didn't think about the cramped room, or the hell chasing them, or the bed that he could have her on in five seconds.

He only thought about her.

She was tight and he pulled back before surging inside her again, her husky moan tripping down his spine like a caress. Her hands gripped the back of his head, nails biting into his skin, and it wasn't enough.

With every stroke, she gripped him tighter, straining against him, her eyes dark and wide, locked on his. He caught one hip, lifted her.

Then, watching her, he stroked. The need to take her harder, ride her until they both lost themselves, was brutal, but he had a stronger need.

The need to chase away the darkness in her eyes. A darkness *he* had brought into her life.

A need to make this last, because it was the sweetest pleasure he'd felt in ages...maybe ever.

A broken sob trembled in the air and he dipped his head, brushed his mouth across her lips, once. Twice.

"I want to feel you come," he whispered against her

lips.

Her breath caught and hitched and her eyes gazed into his with hunger...and hesitation.

It was that look, that feminine look of nerves and need, that let him wrap the reins around the vicious cut of his desire. Shoving away from the wall, he took the few short steps to the bed and then went to his back. Her lush curves, her solid weight, had every nerve in his body singing, but he didn't flip her to her back and drive into her.

Urging her upright, he said, "Ride me, Nyrene."

A blush pinkened her cheeks. Then, with her teeth sinking into her lower lip, she braced her hands against his chest and started to move.

It was a slow, awkward rhythm at first, but after a few seconds that had his eyes crossing, she found her pace. The sensation of her hips rolling on his, the snug clasp of her pussy around his cock, had Dev groaning.

As he arched up to meet her, he gazed at her, imprinting the sight of her, the feel of her, on his memory. Her breasts, those large, soft breasts, were pushed forward by the position of her arms, and the sight of her tight nipples—a warm, delicious brown—had him tangling one hand in her hair, tugging her down.

Nyrene whimpered and then she cried out as he licked her right nipple in a slow, lazy circle before drawing it into his mouth.

He scraped his teeth lightly over the sensitive skin. An excited gasp escaped her lips.

She fell forward. Her nipple popped out of his mouth and he tipped his head back, staring into her eyes—dark and dazed.

With her elbows braced by his shoulders, she started to move. He drove up, matching her rhythm.

The sound of flesh slapping against flesh filled the room, her ragged sighs mingling with his low groan.

He felt it start, her climax, and he lashed down the need to come. Her muscles went tight, her body barely moving now. Gripping her hip in one hand, he held her tightly against him and thrust.

She keened, a low, desperate sound—his name.

She said his name as she came and it was too much. Dev caught her mouth with his as he orgasmed, the bliss of it, of *her*, ripping all threads of control from him.

She had never felt that...replete.

Not once in her life.

She'd come close, maybe, or something that resembled close, but it required the use of the showerhead and lots of dirty little fantasies for her to come.

Nyrene suspected Dev had all but ruined her for the showerhead.

"I want to do that again."

She didn't even realize she'd spoken until Dev brushed his lips over her neck. "Give me a few minutes and we can definitely do that again."

Blushing, she tucked her face against him. Embarrassment twisted inside her, but it paled in comparison to that anticipation that had her shivering against him.

One strong, rough hand stroked down her back.

She sighed, feeling more relaxed than she had felt in days.

Since before the wreck, even.

That wreck had tripped off everything, but she'd been uneasy for days. She'd worried about her boyfriend for days, and that nagging sensation in her gut was what had her driving by the day she saw him tangling tongues with his new hire.

Now, though, all of that was gone. Her head didn't hurt. Her thoughts were clear.

And—

Have to hurry. They'll leave before dawn and I don't want to try to chase them down again.

She sucked in a breath and twisted away from Dev, drawing her knees to her chest.

Eyes closed, she felt it pressing against her head— thoughts that weren't her own, emotions she couldn't understand.

Cold. Calculating.

This is a lot of money, boys. Our objective is to grab her and if we can keep from scaring her, even better. It's going to be hard, but if she freaks out and shuts down, it makes the boss's job harder. Let's keep the boss happy.

Grab *her*. They mean *me*.

There were no faces in her mind this time, no scenes of death and blood playing out.

Just those cool, calculating thoughts.

"Nyrene!"

The urgency in Dev's voice was as effective as a bucket of cold water.

Lifting her lashes, she stared at him.

"We have to leave. *Now.*"

CHAPTER TWELVE

Dev didn't believe in wasting time and he didn't believe in questioning instinct.

This time, it was somebody else's instincts—or whatever he'd call some weird psychic shit—but it didn't change the rules of the game.

That had been fear in Nyrene's eyes and fear required a response. This time, it was flight.

He wanted, more than anything, to stay and *fight*, but as long as he was watching over her, then she came first. Before his need to inflict vengeance, before his need to track down whoever was hunting her.

He'd find a way to make her safe and *then* he'd deal with everything else.

They pulled out of the parking lot less than ten minutes after Nyrene had told him they had to leave, and every second of the time between he'd kept one eye on the door.

Almost five miles lay between them and the motel before he spoke.

"Are we okay?"

She stared ahead into the darkness. "How would I know?"

With a short laugh, Dev said, "How would you *not* at this point? You've been right every other time."

She sighed and looked away. "Yeah, right. *Lucky.* Luck doesn't last. What are we supposed to do, Dev? We can't just run forever."

He ran his tongue along his teeth and then reached into his shirt pocket. "Here."

Nyrene glanced at him and the card he held, but she didn't take it.

"She wrote something on the back."

"She wants me to call her," Nyrene said. "That's *insane.*"

"None of the stuff going on right now makes a lot of sense, and you need to find somebody who can help you make sense of it. She seems like a damn good bet, if you ask me." He paused and then added softly, "This seems like a lousy thing to try to handle on your own."

Slowly, she took the card. "I was looking for answers, you know," she said, her voice reluctant. "I'd been doing some digging around online the night you..."

She hesitated.

Tightening his hands on the steering wheel, Dev muttered, "The night I showed up and scared the shit out of you."

There wasn't any response, but he didn't see much of a need for one. They both knew what he'd done.

"Did you have any luck finding anything?"

Nyrene scraped the tip of her nail over the simple black font on the card. "I don't know. I'd found this one site—they called it The Psychic Portal, but everything went crazy before I could really talk to anybody. Honestly, I'd rather talk to somebody from there than Taige Morgan. She's..."

"Strange," Dev said when Nyrene hesitated yet again. "And yeah, I understand. But look at it this way. She's a known quantity. She works with the FBI and has..." He grimaced, because he still couldn't believe he was actually *talking* about this. *Once you eliminate the impossible,* he reminded himself. And they'd pretty much done that. "Morgan has closed who knows how many cases. Seems to me she's a safer bet than talking to people you don't know."

"Yeah."

When she said nothing else, he turned over the throwaway cell phone and waited for her to take it.

Slowly, she did.

* * * * *

Oman came out of the motel room, struggling to keep

his cool.

He was damn glad he hadn't put together any sort of team for this, but there was no way he would have risked that. How could he, considering he was dealing with an unknown in this equation?

The clerk at the motel had recognized a picture that Oman had shown to him of Deverall, although he claimed not to have seen a woman.

The strange female who had approached Oman out of the blue had walked around the room, the clicking of her heels muffled on the thin, fraying shag carpet. He'd overheard her talking to the three men who'd been in the truck with her.

"They're gone. We barely missed them, but they are gone. Find me something."

Then she'd turned and focused a broad smile on him.

"We were close. We'll do better next time, but I need to know if you can help me with something."

Oman's gut said to stay the hell away from the woman.

But somehow, she'd managed to track down Deverall to this motel when nothing Oman had done had panned out. She wasn't a cop, so he had no concerns she might be working with the federal agent who'd almost busted his very much deceased partner, but she had an angle. He just needed to figure out what it was.

"I might be able to help. I might not."

She continued to watch him with that bright, winning smile.

"You've got a cop watching the house of the woman your boy is with. I just need him to...not be quite so alert for a few hours. I need one of my people to slip inside that house for a little while."

"And just why do you need that?"

"You don't need to worry about it," one of the men with her said, coming up from behind him. When he spoke, he clapped a hand over the back of Oman's neck. "Now do you?"

Oman's brain went hazy. He blinked as he studied the woman in front of him, his thoughts falling out of place. Did he? "Do I what?" he asked.

"Lieutenant Oman," the woman said, swaying closer, "we need your help to find this cop...and we really need your help to find the woman he's with. She'll cause you a lot of trouble. Why don't you just let us get her out of your hair?"

"It's a good idea." The man behind him squeezed Oman's neck gently.

"Yes." Oman nodded. "It is a good idea."

He never even thought to question his easy acquiescence or why he so suddenly felt like it was just a good idea to trust the woman in front of him. He, who tended to trust people about as far as he could throw them, would have happily turned over his weapon to the pretty, smiling blonde in that moment, had she asked him.

It did occur to her, but they would benefit more having somebody around who could answer questions or maybe clear the legal tape if any arose.

Besides, these cops had made such a mess already, killing another one just might be the straw that broke the camel's back.

Giving him a coaxing smile, she nodded at the phone on his belt. "Why don't you call that cop who's watching her house? We've got a guy in place who can take care of what we need and we'll be that much closer to getting out of your hair then."

*   *   *   *   *

The man's smile was just as easy as it had been a few days ago. Nyrene couldn't help but notice that.

His gaze slid from her to Dev and then back before he pushed off the car and came toward them.

Before she could figure out what to say, Dev was already talking.

"You." The menace in Dev's voice would have given *her* pause.

The man, with his heavy shoulders and roughly cut features, just lifted a brow.

"Me," he replied, his tone just as easy as his smile. He dipped his head in Dev's direction, then nodded at Nyrene. "The name is Crawford. Special Agent Joss Crawford, FBI. I'm a friend of Taige Morgan's. She's aware that you've got a...situation going on. I'm a little more mobile right now than she is, so...here I am." He held out his arms and offered a cocky smile. It faded quickly, though, and he slanted a look at Nyrene. "How is your head?"

She blinked. "My head?" Then she remembered, reaching up to touch the still-aching bruise that bloomed on her face like an ugly flower. She'd all but forgotten about *that*. Impossible as it was to believe, the pain from being struck had paled in comparison to everything else.

Considering how bad things could get, she guessed it wasn't a surprise.

With a shrug, she said, "It hurts. I'll live."

"It hurts..." He studied her face for a long moment and then nodded. "And yeah, you'll live. I was talking more about the mess you've got suddenly brewing up there, though." He tapped his forehead.

Nyrene flushed. *Mess* seemed too simplistic a description. "I don't know," she said. "Part of me is just hoping this is some bad dream and I'll wake up normal."

"What in the hell is normal?" He shrugged off the idea. "So...you talked to Taige. But something tells me that didn't do much other than bring about more questions."

Nyrene nodded, looking away from him to stare at the bustling, crowded parking lot. "Yeah. We only had a few minutes. We've got these..." She licked her lips and looked over at Dev before meeting Joss's eyes once more, uncertain how he'd react if she told him that they'd had to leave the highway and Taige had been the one to abruptly shout, *Turn left!* "We didn't have long," she finished lamely.

Joss eyed her appraisingly as she thought about the short, terse interval she'd had with Taige Morgan—a woman known pretty much throughout the entire country at this point. They called her the Psychic of the South. There had been a TV documentary done on her, not that she'd participated or appeared on it, but it was all about cases she'd solved, lives she'd saved. Some of the stories went back to when she'd been little more than a child.

The conversation had ended abruptly with Taige's demanding shout—*Turn left!* Instinct had kicked in and Dev had done that, while Nyrene's brain went into overdrive.

Her heart had been racing, her head spinning, but everything had gone eerily, icily cold in the next moment as the loud, staccato blasts filled the air.

Somebody had started shooting at them.

They'd been found—again.

As though he knew exactly what she was thinking, Dev reached down and caught her hand, squeezing gently.

She squeezed back and when he went to pull away, she didn't let go.

Joss continued to eye her narrowly for a long, tense moment. "She warned you about the Portal, right? You need to stay away from there, not talk to *anybody* who tries to contact you from there."

"Yeah." Rubbing the heel of her hand over her chest, Nyrene wished she could undo the past few days, or even those few minutes when she'd gone poking around on the website. "How can they be tracking me? I didn't tell them *anything*."

Joss was quiet so long, she didn't know if he'd answer.

But then, slowly, he held out a hand.

She stared at his broad palm and then slowly accepted it.

Immediately, all the clamor in her head faded away.

Just like that.

There was no noise—she'd lived with nothing *but* noise in her head since these headaches had started right after the wreck. She'd thought that *window* trick had been helping, but...no. It was like using a paper bag to block the rain.

For the first time in days, she had silence in her head and no pain.

"How..." She sucked in a breath. "How did you do that?"

"Practice." He squeezed her hand when she would have pulled back. "You're already figuring it out, aren't you? What are you using?"

Confused, she stared at him.

"You block out the voices you hear," Joss said, clarifying. "How?"

"A...um, a window," she replied, glancing at Dev before looking back at Joss. This was all insane. How could she be standing here with him like this, talking about this as if it was...*real?*

"You need something stronger." His mouth went tight. "A window that you can open and close isn't bad...if you're run-of-the-mill, but Nyrene, you light up like neon. You're not run-of-the-mill. Taige said you were in a wreck, right?"

Numb, Nyrene nodded, trying to understand what he was getting at.

"Chances are you've always had...we'll call it *good instincts*. You know when to take an umbrella even on sunny days, for example, don't you?"

Mystified, she asked, "What's that got to do with anything?"

"If the weatherman says no rain, and the sky is blue, why are you taking an umbrella?" He waited for a response. "And when you do, does it rain?"

She held up her hands. "How should I know? I don't count rainy days versus sunny days!"

"But it's happened." He nodded, looking satisfied. "I'd bet you know when to get off the highway, and you find out after you got off there was a bad wreck a few miles up, right?"

Nyrene swiped her hands down her pants. Okay, so maybe she could recall a few times when that had happened. Maybe. "That doesn't mean anything," she said, her voice shaking.

"Not by itself." Joss squeezed her hand again and she wondered why it didn't feel odd to be standing there in a parking lot with a strange man while he squeezed her hand and asked her asinine questions. Or *odder*. "But if you pair it up with other things?" He leaned in then, voice intense. "You know what I think?"

She swallowed, unable to speak.

"You were always like this, but it was...quieter. You knew certain people were just...no good, didn't you?"

"No!" she fired back. "My ex-boyfriend was a two-timing son of a bitch— No, a *three*-timing son of a bitch. He's married for crap's sake! With kids!"

"Being psychic doesn't come with a guarantee," he said, lips crooking up in a smile. "Some people are just harder for us to read. Especially somebody untrained. Can you honestly tell me that there was never *anybody* who you just knew you should stay away from?"

Licking her lips, Nyrene thought back and she had to shake her head. "No." There actually had been any number of people who had filled her with such...loathing, she'd steered far clear of them. Then, as a rush of understanding hit her, she flinched.

"What is it?" Dev and Joss both asked at once.

"I..." She licked her lips. "I used to call CPS. At my job. We had a couple of parents that I *knew* were hurting their kids, but we had no proof."

Heat flooded her cheeks and she looked away, clearing her throat before speaking. "I'd report them, but without any logical evidence..." Her voice trailed away as she thought about what she'd done.

Finally, she cleared her throat. "I called on the one who bothered me the most, finally. I called and I lied and said I'd heard screaming—a little boy's—coming from the house, begging for help. I lied and said I'd heard it several times."

"And...?" Joss asked.

"We didn't see him for almost a year, but he came back in...with foster parents. They were planning to adopt him." Eyes burning, she looked at Joss for a long moment, then finally over at Dev. "His dad used to touch him. I'm not sorry for what I did. It *saved* him."

Dev gave a short nod, saying nothing.

"So, you've always been like this," Joss said again. "But this wreck...it broke something open inside you. A gate, or maybe a window." He crooked a grin at her. "And now you're wide open."

"What?"

"You're too strong, or your gift is. We'll get into that later. For now, can I?" He squeezed her hand again.

She went to ask what and then jerked back, feeling something *nudge* her...inside her head.

He still held her hand and she tried to twist away at the alien sensation.

"Let her go," Dev said, his voice a growl.

"Not yet." Joss didn't even look away from her. "I'm not hurting you, Nyrene. I won't look at anything—"

Dev went to grab him.

Nyrene *saw* him moving—

And then freezing. Midstep. His face went red, and to her horror, she could see his throat *move*—inward.

Like some unseen hand had grabbed him. "Ease back, Sherlock," Joss said, his voice grim. "I'm not going to hurt her, but she can't function if she doesn't get some sort of hold on this."

Dev's eyes bulged as he clawed at his neck, leaving

SHILOH WALKER

scratches that soon grew red with blood as he fought his way free.

"What are you doing?" Nyrene demanded. To her shock, she'd fisted the man's shirt in her hand—her free one—and she was shaking him.

"Holding him off for a minute so he doesn't beat my ass." Joss's eyes glowed. "I don't have time to coddle you through this. Now are you going to *let* me..."

She sucked in a breath when he nudged her head again, and that unseen touch was his. With a groan, she let him...although she didn't know *what* she was allowing.

In the next moment, Dev hit the floor, his breath sawing in and out. He was up on his feet a second later, but Nyrene held up a hand. "Don't," she whispered bleakly. She couldn't understand why, but this was something she *needed.*

"That's it," Joss murmured. "Now...pay attention. *Feel* what I'm doing."

She couldn't do anything else. It was as if he was laying bricks in her mind.

"A wall," she whispered. "A wall, not a window."

"Exactly. You decide what comes through. But for now, you have to block out almost all of it, Nyrene. You practically glow in the dark."

Bit by bit, everything inside her mind seemed to...change.

But it wasn't just mentally. There were physical changes, too.

She breathed easier.

She felt lighter.

When he finally withdrew that light mental touch, she swayed, then sagged.

Dev caught her, wrapping one arm around her waist. She braced automatically for the onslaught of memories and images, but nothing was there.

"I can't feel anything from you," she said wonderingly as she looked up at him.

Dev's confusion was clear on his face. But she didn't explain. She was too confused, herself. Turning her head, she met Joss's gaze. "How did you do that?"

"It was more you than me," he said, shrugging. "Once your mind realized what I was doing, it sort of took over. I was just guiding things. You needed better shielding. I just helped you figure it out."

His gaze flicked to Dev and he cocked a brow, tossing the man an arrogant grin. "Now, maybe the three of us can get out of here and talk shop?"

* * * * *

Joss's version of *getting out of there* meant relocating to a popular chain steakhouse that served peanuts in the shell and had the warm, yeasty scent of bread drifting out the door.

It had Nyrene's stomach rumbling and she pressed a hand to her belly, hoping to quell the noise. It didn't work. But then again, she and Dev had been a little too focused on staying alive the past few days to worrying much about eating.

"This isn't smart," Dev said as they went through the doors. "There's a BOLO out on me, and probably here, too, at this point."

"Oh, those are being dealt with," Joss said, his voice unconcerned.

"What?"

But Dev's question went unanswered as they passed through a busy crush of people in the waiting area and on into the bar where they found, miraculously, an empty booth.

Joss took it, settling in the middle of one bench while waiting for them to take the other. Waylon Jennings wailed on the radio and Joss gestured to the room in general. "It's loud," he said, leaning forward. Voice pitched so they had no trouble hearing it, but low enough Nyrene had no doubt that nobody else *would* hear him, he continued. "And it's Friday. People here are enjoying a drink after the end of the week, getting ready to go home. Nobody is likely to be paying attention to you guys. Except maybe cops, and nobody is getting off shift any time soon. It's the middle of the evening." He tapped his watch, then looked up just as a woman stopped at the end of the booth.

They placed orders for drinks and when the server came to Nyrene, she said, "Whiskey. Whatever you got, a double. Straight up."

Normally, she wasn't a drinker, but she needed some

damn alcohol right then.

Joss gave her a sympathetic look. "It's a lot to take in," he said after the woman made her way back into the crowd.

"Excuse me,"—Dev gave her an apologetic look—"but I need to know. What the hell did you mean by 'it's being taken care of'? BOLOs don't just disappear because some FBI agent shows up."

"Nah, that has nothing to do with me. There's a bigger fish than me pulling strings and I imagine he's putting some weight behind it." Joss gave a thin smile. "It probably has something to do with the fact that your department is dirtier than a couple of contenders after a bout of mud wrestling."

Dev arched his brows then, leaning back as he studied Joss appraisingly. "They've caught federal interest."

"They have now." Joss gave him a shark's smile. "They fucked with me and that caught my interest. I did some digging around. An awful lot of cops die in your neck of the woods, do you know that? And the murder rate in your little city...it's kind of crazy."

"I'm aware," Dev bit off.

The words sounded jagged and rusty to Nyrene's ears.

"I've sent a report to the Louisiana Bureau of Investigation, but who the fuck knows how long it will be before they get to me?" Now Dev just sounded frustrated. "And good cops keep dying. Decent people die when they end up stumbling into something they shouldn't."

His eyes flickered and she knew he was thinking of Meredith and her fiancé.

"I suspect the LBI will find your file much sooner than you think. They're getting a call from Taige," Joss said softly.

From the corner of her eye, Nyrene could see the way Dev's mouth tightened, but then, to her surprise, he gave a short, stiff nod. "From what I hear, she makes a phone call and people jump to attention," Dev said softly.

"That's because when she makes a call, she has solid-gold information." Joss shrugged. "I'm a cop, too, Deverall. I like closing cases just as much as you do. Once some agent at the LBI takes a look at this, realizes cops are getting killed, innocent citizens dying...? You'll be the next one to get a phone call. Don't be surprised if you end up getting a job offer to get you out of that armpit of a town, either. LBI's always looking for good cops."

There was another lull in the conversation as the server reappeared, distributing a round of drinks and asking if they needed any food. Joss answered for them all with a polite, "Can we just flag you down when we need you?"

Once they were alone again, he leaned back over the table. "In the meantime, the good mayor of Clary is getting a call from my boss. He's going to be told that we're aware that some...odd information is being passed around about an informant of ours, one Benjamin Deverall. We'd be mighty upset if anything happened to one of ours, you know." His eyes caught and held Dev's. "The BOLO is going to be dropped, probably within the hour. If not, I'll be in touch so you know to keep watching your backs on that front."

"The men after me aren't going to stop just because the mayor got goosed by the FBI. For all I know, the mayor is in it up to his neck."

"He's not." Joss shook his head. "Before the head man in charge got on the phone with him, one of our empaths spoke with the mayor. He's a self-serving bastard, but he's not dirty. Also, your captain has her suspicions about what's going on in the department. She's safe to talk to."

Safe to talk to.

Bewildered, Dev looked at the man sitting across from him. He didn't know what to make of *any* of this. He knew all about trusting his gut, which was where he was going to file what Nyrene could do—she just had seriously sharp instincts and he was going to make himself be okay with that.

But now he had a man he didn't know from Adam telling him something that *his* gut had suspected for a long time, but to his knowledge, Joss Crawford didn't know the lieutenant. "I'm sorry," he finally said. "How do you know *any* of this shit?"

"We're the FBI," Joss said soberly. "We know everything."

But the joke fell flat. Not just for him, he realized, but for Nyrene.

"How do they know about *me?*" she asked, her voice urgent. "I don't understand any of this. How did Taige know about me? How was anybody from this so-called Psychic Portal able to track me? Because I...what? You say I glow in the dark? And because of that, they sent you here? Why? Why do *I* matter to the FBI?"

Joss studied them both, irritation stamped on his features. He blew out a breath and finally he reached for his phone. "I need you two to cooperate with me if I want anything accomplished, and I want several things accomplished. One, I want your laptop, Nyrene. You're our first solid lead on the Portal in a while and we need that lead. Two..." His eyes flicked to Dev and he shrugged. "Dirty cops piss me off." He tapped something out on the phone, then put it face down on the table. "But I'm not going to get much cooperation if I don't garner some trust."

The phone buzzed almost immediately.

"So I'm going to attempt to garner some trust." He picked up the phone. But he didn't look at it immediately. "But I'll tell you this now—if you fuck me over or do anything to upset the person you might be getting ready to meet? You're going to be dealing not just with me, you'll deal with somebody a lot scarier." He looked down at the phone and his mouth tightened. "She said yes. Come on, we need to pay and get out of here before she changes her mind."

"What are you talking about?" Dev asked.

But Joss didn't answer. He was fishing bills out of his wallet. After a cursory glance at the table—*Tallying up the tab*, Dev thought—he tossed down a few bills, then added another ten. "Come on," he said again, sounding impatient.

"I'd like to know *where* first." Dev stayed stubbornly where he was.

"I think I know," Nyrene said weakly.

Dev looked over at her and saw she'd fisted a hand by her head.

"Keep that wall up, Nyrene," Joss said, his voice hard.

"I am. This...it's just there." She held up a hand, as if grasping for an explanation in thin air. She looked at Dev, then back at Joss. "You're taking us to meet Taige, aren't you?"

Joss's mouth tightened.

"Taige," she whispered. "And her daughter."

CHAPTER THIRTEEN

She was...delicate.

That was the only word that accurately described the slim, petite girl waiting next to the tall woman Nyrene immediately pegged as Taige Morgan. And there was *nothing* delicate about Taige.

Everything about the woman hailed as the Psychic of the South screamed confidence and quiet, determined capability. Nyrene had the idea that someone could hand her the drawn-out plans to bring about WWIII and she'd just nod and go about thwarting them all without breaking a sweat.

Oddly enough, although she was clearly still a teenager, the girl next to Taige carried herself with the same confidence, the same strength.

And Nyrene saw it—these two weren't mother and daughter by blood—but they were in every other way.

Taige was mixed-race, like Nyrene herself. It was there in the pale gold of her skin, the pale gray of her eyes and the crazy curls she'd pulled back from her face in a series of braids.

Jillian, on the other hand, was petite and fair. Her hair was curly, too, but the curls were loose and soft, framing her face in a series of ringlets. Her mouth looked like a cupid's bow, pink and perfect and completely naked of lipstick. Her eyes were big and dark, an inky shade of blue that made Nyrene think of midnight as she approached.

The top of her head came up to Nyrene's chin but she held the older woman's gaze steadily, her slender shoulders ramrod straight, her gaze appraising.

Abruptly, her mother's lips curled up and Taige looked away, her gaze drifting down to her daughter's. "Stop that, baby."

Jillian Morgan hadn't done a thing.

But she shrugged. "Sorry."

"Don't apologize to *me*," Taige said, nudging her.

Jillian's gaze flitted to Nyrene and she sighed. "Fine. I'm sorry." Then she pursed her lips and added, "But I'm *not* delicate."

Joss covered a laugh with a cough as Nyrene's steps stumbled to a halt. "Maybe I should have mentioned something. Jillian can read minds. *Any* mind—whether it's shielded or not. The gift is sort of spiking out of control right now, too, so she can't always control it."

"Maybe you should *try* harder," Nyrene snapped immediately, and instinctively, doubling the wall that Joss had built inside her mind.

Jillian opened her mouth to reply, then she stopped, face scrunching up. "How did you do that?" she demanded.

"Do what?" Nyrene crossed her arms over her chest, feeling oddly naked.

"You..." Jillian waved a hand at Nyrene's head. "You just knocked me out of your head. *Nobody* can do that."

While Nyrene struggled to answer, Taige refocused her gaze on Nyrene. After a few short moments, a smile spread across her face. "Oh, honey...I think I'm going to like you."

"Mom!"

* * * * *

"As long as you keep yourself locked up tight like you are now, you don't need to worry about people from the Portal finding you." Taige looked at Nyrene and shook her head. "If Jillian can't pick up on you, it's like you don't even exist."

Nyrene slid a look over to the girl in question. "I don't want to say I'm doubting you but..."

"You are doubting me," Taige said.

"She's a kid," Nyrene responded. She grimaced and looked at Jillian. "No offense."

Jillian rolled her eyes. "Anytime somebody says no

offense, there's usually offense."

"Jillian, I've told you about rolling your eyes," Taige said.

"I'm not even looking at you." Jillian made a face.

"I can hear it in your voice," the woman said, glancing at the girl from the corner of her eye. "And you heard me." Her gaze shifted back to Nyrene. "I know it's hard to get, but Jillian is...well... If you haven't seen her in action, you won't get it. But her gift came on her when she was a small child. Half the cases in recent years that are attributed to me were actually solved because she gave me the lead."

She laughed at the expression on Nyrene's face. "And those are just the ones that leaked out into the public eye. There are more that will never see the light of day. She looks, and is currently acting like a normal teenage girl, but she's seen and dealt with things no seventeen-year-old— hell, no twenty-year— No fifty-seven-year-old should ever have to see."

Nyrene swallowed, because the expression on Taige's face had taken on a dark cast. Jillian slid her hand into her mother's and the two of them shared a private moment.

It was shattered by Dev as he said, "Look, I don't want to discount you, Jillian...or you, Ms. Morgan, but these characters are showing up out of nowhere. Nyrene's barely had a chance to give us warning most of the time and we've had to haul ass so often, I would have sworn that she had some sort of GPS on her."

Nyrene couldn't stop herself from sending him a disgruntled look.

He caught sight of it, too. She could tell by the dull flush that showed up along his cheekbones. He had acted in a way that was almost absurdly gentle ever since he had come to the conclusion that she was telling the truth. Well, save for that one time...

There had been nothing gentle about the way his hands had flown over her body. Nothing gentle in the way his mouth took hers.

She fought the urge to shiver.

"Ah...Nyrene?" Taige said. She coughed, covering her mouth with her fist and slid a look at her daughter. The teenager was standing there with wide eyes and a pink flush to her pretty face.

Nyrene realized she had dropped the shield she had

somehow managed to erect and she slammed in back into place.

Jillian shook her head, looking a bit dazed. "I don't know how you do that. That wall you have is a tight piece of work," the girl commented, sounding old beyond her years.

"Can you really pick up on everybody?" But she wasn't looking at Jillian.

Rather, she looked at Taige, and although she had her shield up tight, Taige must have picked up on what she was thinking. Her smile was understanding. "People might not be able to block Jillian, but she can block people. And after a while, once she gets used to somebody, they become background noise to her, even if they are...unusually strong."

Nyrene shook her head. "Still...all the time?" She tried to imagine being assailed by the images that came at her all the time and she thought she'd go crazy if she had to deal with that.

Something of what she felt must have shown on her face, because Jillian crooked a grin at her. "When you live with it all the time, you learn to cope a lot faster. Really, it's all I've ever known. I don't remember a time when my mind was completely my own. There's always been...voices or scenes. Something up here." She wiggled her fingers near her temple.

Nyrene felt an insane urge to hug the girl.

Unaware of what Nyrene was thinking, she said, "It's different with you, from what I saw before you shut me out. You're still hit-or-miss and it seems more..." Jillian paused, clearly searching for the right way to phrase it. "Situational with you. You react to people you know are in danger, and for things that affect you directly."

"Not always," Nyrene said, thinking of the reporter. She explained.

"But that did, or would have, affected you. Dev was important to your safety." Taige glanced at him. "If he had been...arrested, that would have affected you."

"Arrested, Mom?" Jillian said, her tone sardonic.

She knew, Nyrene realized abruptly. This seventeen-year-old girl knew all the dark, ugly truths that Nyrene had been dealing with. But she was already struggling to deal with what she was learning, what she had already learned, so she pushed that realization to the side. "How could that have affected me?" she asked. She shot Dev a look, then, deciding to say the hell with subtly, she pointed out, "I'm in trouble *because* of him."

Dev's face tightened, but he said nothing.

"There's a connection, still. Either between you and him," Taige said, her eyes moving between the two of them tellingly. "Or between you and those who set this reporter up to be killed. I don't know. You may not ever know. But that connection is there."

The memory of his hands on her, his skin sliding back and forth over hers, his body so hard, hungry and taut as he rode her, flashed through her mind. But Nyrene quelled the thought before it could lead to another.

"What are we to do?" she asked, voice husky. "I can't even begin to go back to a normal life right now. I don't know if I *ever* can. There are cops looking for me now. And you say that as long as I can stay shielded, these freaks from The Psychic Portal—"

"You're one of the freaks now, too," Jillian pointed out.

"I'm not trying to stalk and kidnap myself," Nyrene replied with a quick glance at the girl. Redirecting her attention back to the other woman, she said, "But I don't know if I *can* keep this shield up—I have to concentrate to do it and it's..." She rubbed her temples. "It's exhausting."

She already felt as if she had sand rubbing on the inside of her brain. She'd adjusted to the pressure and fatigue that came with maintaining that window, but she didn't know how long it would take to adjust to holding this wall that Joss had built inside her mind. She'd done full-body workouts that didn't wear her out as much as it did to hold up this mental...wall.

"It's because it's new." Taige came closer and held up her hands, palms facing each other. "May I?"

Nyrene eyed her warily. "Any time somebody touches me, weird shit goes off in my head."

"Did you get weird shit when Joss touched you?" she asked. "Well, other than how he helped you build that wall."

Nyrene's lids flickered as she thought back. "Well, no."

"You won't with me, neither," she said. "Promise."

Cool fingertips touched Nyrene's temples and Taige gently said, "This ability you have, it requires control—a lot of it. It takes practice, like an athlete learning a new skill or a dancer learning a new routine."

Taige's eyes went smoky and opaque. "You are...strong, Nyrene. I can't believe you've been quiet this long."

"Quiet?"

Taige blinked and her eyes cleared. "That your gift hasn't emerged until now. That wreck..." She laughed. "Trauma will do it but whether it was the emotional trauma of finding out about your boyfriend, the emotional trauma from the wreck, the physical trauma from said wreck, or all of the three, something knocked down whatever it was that kept your gift quiet and now it's like it's screaming." Taige lowered her hands and stepped back. "I can help you. And you, in turn, can help me."

"How can I help you?" Nyrene asked, dismayed.

Taige's lips curved. "They are hunting you because you sent an email. I'd like you to send another...unshielded. I'll be there with you, and so will Jillian and Joss."

"Why?"

"Because we've been hunting these sons of bitches for several years now and you're the one person we've come across who has had contact who hasn't been grabbed by them."

"You want to set a trap for them," Nyrene said, her voice raw. "And I'm the bait."

"In a sense," Taige agreed. "But you will only be bait in the simplest of terms. Once that email is sent, you will not be anywhere near where they can find you. You'll be at my facility, protected. I'll have my people protecting you."

"Your people," Dev said slowly. "Does that mean the FBI?"

"No." Taige slanted a look at him. "I'm not with the FBI anymore. I run a private security group. However, the FBI and I are both interested in apprehending somebody from this group who is attempting to capture you, Nyrene. They are dangerous. They need to be stopped, and you're quite right. You won't be safe until that happens."

"This sounds a lot like blackmail," Dev said, disgusted. "You'll offer protection as long as she helps you out."

"You're a cop. What protection do you offer material witnesses?" Taige cocked a brow at him. She looked back at Nyrene and said, "I will teach you how to better protect yourself, but I can't have you at my facility unless you're willing to help me stop the bloodhounds after you, Nyrene. I won't endanger the people I have there. Some of them are...fragile. Fragile in ways you wouldn't understand, and I have a responsibility to them."

"If you weren't planning on helping her, why the fuck did you even set up a meeting?" Dev demanded.

"Stop it," Nyrene said, stepping between them, hands held up. "Just...stop, okay, Dev? She's right. I hate it, but she's right. I can't even begin to think about going back to my life until I know these people aren't going to be dogging me." Taking a deep breath, she focused on Taige. "So...what do we do first?"

Joss cleared his throat. "First, we make sure that BOLO is taken care of, then we deal with your little problem in Clary."

"But..." Nyrene looked from him to Taige, then over at Dev.

Dev stared hard at Joss, though, for a long moment, before nodding. "You said the BOLO was expected to be called off by nightfall. But regardless, cops have ways. Connections." He looked over at Nyrene. "We have to take care of the cops because, if we don't, whoever is after you could very well use law enforcement to track you."

"Exactly."

CHAPTER FOURTEEN

Oman faced off with the captain.

"I'm just trying to figure out why the BOLO was called off Deverall and this chick he's been spotted with," he said, spreading his hands out wide. "None of us think he's dirty, but he's running and that doesn't look good. Plus, somebody set his house to blow, Captain! He's in trouble!"

He thought he'd put the right amount of frustration and worry into his voice. He hoped.

He'd asked around, subtly, hoping to get answers as to why the BOLO had abruptly been canceled, but nobody he'd talked to knew anything.

The captain was the next person on the ladder and if she didn't have answers, he was going to have to talk to his boss. He was a little leery of doing that, because so far, he hadn't heard from the boss, which meant he hadn't had to give an update.

That did *not* mean the boss didn't know about the lack of progress.

Sadly, the boss seemed to know everything before it even happened, although how that was possible, Oman didn't know.

"I can't help you out here, Oman. I know you want to solve this case, but word came down from on high and that's all I can say," Captain Clair Amana said, not even looking up at him from the reports she was reading.

It seemed as if the mountain of them had grown in the few days since he'd been in her office and he imagined her tripping, falling, being buried under an avalanche of paper, suffocating under them.

If he didn't have to deal with her straight-laced, stickup-the-ass ways, his life would be a little easier. Maybe he never would have even had to have gone down the route he went down.

A few too many excessive-force claims and he'd been looking at another unpleasant meeting with his superiors, maybe even a demotion or being removed from the force.

But one meeting had changed everything, and overnight the latest claim of excessive force had disappeared.

Maybe he should have just quit a few years back, gotten out while the getting was good.

"And you're *okay* with this? A BOLO we called for suddenly just getting brushed aside?" he demanded.

The captain lifted her head. She was a few years younger than he was, although he looked as if he had her by a decade, easily. Yet, there was steel in her spine and in her eyes as she met his gaze. "I don't think I'm *okay* with your tone, Lieutenant."

"I apologize," he bit off. One of these days, *he* would be the one standing behind that fucking desk.

Of course, by then, she'd get another promotion and he'd still have to kiss her fucking ass.

Her phone rang and he lapsed into silence as she took the call, taking a few minutes to clear texts and emails from his phone while she made vague comments to whatever asshole cop she talking to, and there was no doubt she was talking to one of his fellow boys in blue. Why she was trying to be so discreet about it, he had no idea. She should have just told him to step outside. It would have been less obvious.

Finally, she ended the call and he slid his phone back onto the clip at his belt.

"Captain—"

She held up a hand. "If this has to do with the BOLO or Deverall, unless it's something new, you might as well save it, Oman. There's nothing I can tell you."

He snapped his mouth shut so hard, his teeth clicked together audibly.

"Is there anything else, Lieutenant?" she asked softly.

He gave a quick shake of his head, although he had easily another fifty questions he could have fired at her. The reason he didn't? He knew he wouldn't get anywhere with her.

He'd do anything to get *her* out of the way, but while he had some powerful friends, she was the fucking captain and more—she had connections to people that went straight to the capitol.

That made her pretty much off limits.

He'd just have a word with his boss.

What that man didn't already know, he could find out.

It must be good to be the deputy fucking mayor.

* * * * *

"I don't like this idea," Dev said. The small town of Clary spread out in front of them in a sleepy sprawl. He shot Joss a look before turning his eyes to Nyrene. "It's dangerous. It's stupid."

It didn't make him feel any better to see her smooth, golden skin go a little pale at his words.

Joss scowled at him. "Way to breathe a lot of confidence into her, pal." He turned to her, rubbing her shoulder. "It's going to be okay, sweetheart. I wouldn't let you do this and neither would Taige if either of us had doubts that we could take care of you."

Dev wanted to knock the other man's hand away from her. It didn't matter that the guy was just being friendly and trying to make her feel better. It didn't matter that the guy had a wedding ring on.

Normally he wasn't the type to be possessive. But he seemed to have lost his mind a little bit when it came to Nyrene.

Okay. He had lost his mind a lot when it came to Nyrene. Vaguely, he was aware of Joss speaking to her and he tried to make himself concentrate on what was being said, but he couldn't. He was too busy thinking about everything that could go wrong once they let Nyrene climb into the car that Joss had provided for her.

It was a rental and she had gotten it under her name. Joss had provided nothing, not even the funds for her to get the car, although he had said he would reimburse her when she had mentioned that she was tight on money, thanks to losing her job.

Dev didn't know if he'd known that. Had he known she had lost her job? He didn't think she had mentioned it, although it wasn't like they'd had a lot of time for small talk. "I don't like leaving her unprotected," he said, turning back to face Joss.

The big guy returned his gaze levelly. "She's not going to be unprotected. I'm going to be right outside."

"Right. And exactly how are you going to get right outside and how are you going to keep anybody who might be watching the house from seeing you? These are *cops* we're talking about. We might not be FBI," Dev added, his voice sardonic "but we are cops. Small town hicks maybe, but cops nonetheless."

"Trust me, I'm well aware." Joss's smile was hard-edged. "That fact has not escaped me for even a minute. And for the record, if I didn't think you were a *good* cop, and a *capable* one, this wouldn't be happening."

That didn't make him feel any better. Joss knew they were dealing with dirty cops.

"Don't worry about me being noticed." Joss shook his head. "It's not going to happen. My...abilities come in handy in a lot of ways. If anybody is watching that house, I'm going to know it."

"Almost seems like cheating," Dev muttered. He looked at Nyrene and found a resolute expression on her face. Still, he had to try. "You don't have to do this. We can figure out something else."

"Will they come after me?" she asked, a stubborn set to her chin.

He didn't even have to say anything. His expression said at all. He could tell by the way she closed her eyes that she was even now more determined than she had been. "I got pulled into this for a reason," she said. "I'm going to see it through."

Dev wanted to rip out his hair. He wanted to ring Taige's neck, Joss's neck. The echo of her words seemed to coincide with things he'd heard those two say.

Plus...

I'm in trouble because of him, she had said. And those words had been nothing but the stone-cold truth. She was in trouble because of him. That's all there was to it. But standing here and arguing wasn't going to help anything, either. She had made up her mind.

She felt as though she had a part to play and the longer he drew this out, the longer she would be out here exposed to whomever it was who was hunting her. The longer they were both exposed.

The longer it would be before he could protect her.

"Fine," he bit off. "But I want it on record that I think this is a bad idea."

"I know." To his surprise, Nyrene closed the distance between them and rose to her toes. She kissed him on the corner of his mouth. He was hard-pressed not to deepen the kiss but if he put his hands on her, he just might throw her over his shoulder and take her some place where he could keep her safe. But how long could he do that? How long could he keep her safe? He didn't know. And that was the problem. He didn't know.

"Okay." He pulled out his phone and checked the time. "Let's go over this again."

As Nyrene turned away, Joss met his gaze. Something unspoken passed between the two men and Dev didn't have to be psychic to pick up on the message.

I'll take care of her, the man's eyes seem to say.

Dev tightened his hand around his phone.

You sure as hell better.

*   *   *   *   *

"Captain Amana."

The captain's brisk voice came over the phone and Dev didn't have to be there to know the woman would be holding a cup of coffee in one hand and shuffling through reports with the other.

"It's Deverall," he said coolly.

He had to give her credit. He had worried that the second he gave his name she would explode. She was pretty unflappable, but she didn't often have to deal with one of her cops disappearing right after his house blew up. Sure, she'd had an unusual number of cops die on her watch, but she didn't often have them disappear on her.

"Well, the prodigal son," she said.

"Can you talk?"

*   *   *   *   *

Once he was done with the captain, he opened his

messages and sent a text.

Made contact. Will text back soon. Everything good on your end?

His reply came almost immediately.

Smooth sailing. Our girl is in place. She's got one pair of eyes on her place. And let me tell you, guy is lazy AF.

Another message popped up a few seconds later.

Stay Sharp.

Dev sent back a quick response.

You do the same. Take care of her.

That done, he shoved his phone into his pocket and twisted the key in the ignition. Now all he had to do was get his ass to Nyrene's and hope like hell Joss knew what he was doing.

CHAPTER FIFTEEN

Nyrene sat in the car, parked in the gravel driveway in front of her small, rundown house. It was a cozy little place and she'd been fixing it up as best as she could on the paycheck she brought home each week, but she was under no illusions about her home.

She didn't need illusions, either.

It was *home* and it had been a warm, comfortable sanctuary. But right now, it looked ominous, as if a shadow had fallen across the small, single-story, two-bedroom house.

With a hand that shook, she pulled out the pay-as-you-go phone Joss had pushed into her hand only an hour earlier. There were only two numbers programmed into it. One was for an identical phone that was now in Ben's possession. The other was for Joss.

As much as she wanted to call Ben, she didn't.

She punched in a call to Joss and he answered on the first ring.

"Yeah?"

"Somebody's been in my place," she said in a low, hushed voice.

"How can you tell?" he asked.

"I...I don't know. I just *feel* it."

To her relief, he didn't brush it off. "Okay. There's nobody in there now. If there was, I'd know. We don't have much time so you need to get inside. Your cop has already contacted his captain so she's on her way now. He'll be on his way, too. You need to be inside that house when they get here."

She nodded, then, feeling silly, said, "Okay.

Um...where are you?"

"I'm close," he told her. "You're safe, Nyrene, okay?"

She didn't know how she could be, but she didn't argue with him. Disconnecting the call, she slid the phone into her purse and climbed from the car.

Cold chills raced up and down her body as she made her way over the busted sidewalk and her hands shook as she fit the key to the lock. Frustrated, she took a deep breath and managed to still that telltale tremor long enough to unlock the door and slip inside. Once in, she flipped all the locks and stood there, her back pressed to the door as she looked around.

She didn't know what to do now.

She didn't even want to *walk* through her house, knowing that some unknown stranger had been inside her place, doing who knows what.

Why had somebody been in her house?

Who had it been?

The phone rang and she jumped at the sound of it.

She had no idea who could be calling, and she definitely wasn't in the mood to chat, so she stayed where she was, staring at absolutely nothing.

How long would it take for somebody to get there?

Who would get there first?

Easing away from the door, she peeked out through the curtains, once again feeling foolish, but unable to help herself.

The phone went to voicemail and a woman's voice, unfamiliar, filled the air.

"Hello, Nyrene."

A chill raced down Nyrene's back and she jerked away from the window to turn and stare at the phone.

She'd swear that the speaker knew she was there.

"I know you're in the house and I know you can hear me."

Nyrene swallowed, fear suddenly coating her tongue and turning her limbs weak.

"It's Phantom from the Portal. I've been trying to get in contact with you. You're in big trouble and I want to help. Will you pick up the phone?"

Nyrene gave an involuntary shake of her head and shrank back against the door.

A sigh came from the machine next to the phone and

Nyrene closed her eyes.

An image flashed across her closed lids.

A woman with short, pale blonde hair and equally pale blue eyes, leaning against a car. She had a phone pressed to her ear and her mouth opened. Words came from the speaker, but to Nyrene, it was as if she was standing next to the woman, not in the small entryway of her little house.

"I'm trying to help you, Nyrene. You reached out to us, remember? What changed?"

You sent a bunch of goons after me, that's what.

The woman's voice tightened and Nyrene instinctively checked the bricks in the mental wall she had erected. They were all tight and secure.

But the woman had sensed something.

Nyrene could tell.

"You're nervous." The words were soothing. The woman's face, still flickering like a blurred TV screen in Nyrene's mind, was not. "I get that. It's difficult having this shit come on you so hard after a lifetime of being normal. That's why you need help. Plus all this crazy shit with this cop you're on the run with. Honey, he's big trouble, trouble you don't need. You need *us*. Will you just stop running?"

Nyrene had to fight the urge to fling the door open and rush to the car, and take off yet again.

She was here for a reason right now, and she'd made a promise.

"I've got men on the way to your place. It's going to take a while but please, just stay there. We'll take care of you."

The call disconnected.

Nyrene grabbed the phone once more and punched in a text to Joss.

The people who've been chasing me know I'm here. They're coming.

His response was *not* the one she was hoping for.

Hey...that's some cool news. We'll make it a party. Taige is coming, too. Guess she had a feeling.

Nyrene resisted the urge to text him and tell him he was a crazy bastard.

Head's up, Nyrene. You've got a cop coming up the walkway right now. I'm already heading over, ETA two minutes. Calling Dev to let him know. Do not open that door.

Nyrene closed her eyes just as somebody knocked.

* * * * *

Dev read the text and swore.

Then he punched in the captain's number. "There's a cop about to knock on her door," he said in a cutting voice. "Where are you?"

"Less than five minutes away," she said. "Where are you?"

"Same." He felt only slightly better, knowing that Joss was on the scene. He was approaching on foot, but said he was less than two minutes away.

"You got back-up coming, too?" he asked.

"Three officers that I trust," she assured him. "Not including you."

He grunted. "Hurry." Without another word, he ended the call and gripped the steering wheel.

When sirens went off behind him, he ignored them and hit the gas.

Didn't it just figure that somebody would recognize him?

And he had no doubt that had been the case. He'd intentionally been driving just a little above the speed limit so he wouldn't catch anybody's attention. He was also in a rental, the keys turned over by Joss just a few minutes after Nyrene had been provided with transportation, so nobody had recognized the car.

Behind him, the unmarked police car gunned its engine and drew closer.

He ignored it and floored it, whipping around the car in front of him and hanging the right that would take him to Nyrene's place. Tires squealed as the car he'd cut off barely managed to avoid slamming into him.

The cop car stayed right on his bumper and Dev had

no doubt the only reason he wasn't now dodging bullets was the fact that he was in the middle of a fairly populated area of Clary. People watched wide-eyed as he whipped the car around another corner, then hung a left, finally on Nyrene's street.

He saw an unmarked car parked in front of Nyrene's house and almost on the heels of that, a big, unmarked Escalade came around a corner at the end of the street.

The captain's ride.

But he didn't breathe a sigh of relief.

Not yet.

Because while he saw the unmarked cop car in front of Nyrene's house, he didn't see the cop.

CHAPTER SIXTEEN

Nyrene sat on the stairs, clutching her purse to her belly and trying not to shiver with fear.

The cop had just unlocked the door.

He must have been the one who'd been inside her house, and while he was there, he'd helped himself to the spare key she kept in her junk drawer in the kitchen.

He'd unlocked the fucking door, then simply outmuscled her as he pushed it open.

Nyrene was five foot eight and solid, with muscle under her curves, but she wasn't any match for a cop who looked like he just might be able to bench press his own car. Muscles strained against the sleeves of his uniform shirt, roping his arms, and as she watched, they bunched and unbunched.

"We're going to take a ride," he told her.

She swallowed and shook her head. "I'm not going anywhere with you."

"Then I'm going to shoot you in the knee," he informed her, his voice strangely remote. Strange, because his eyes were bouncing around all over the place, refusing to linger on her face for even a minute.

But she didn't take that to mean he didn't mean what he said. She had good reason to believe he *did* mean it— the thoughts were practically spray-painted across his mind in sickly neon green. He didn't want to do it, he'd regret it, but he'd do it nonetheless, because he felt he had no choice.

She had a choice, though.

Her choice was to be stubborn and wait it out because

Joss was close, maybe even already in the house, and Dev was coming. All she had to do was stall.

Deciding to risk it, she removed one lone brick in the wall that protected her mind from his. She could glean the surface thoughts in his mind already, but she needed more.

...can't believe I'm doing this. What's my wife going to think?

...no choice. If I don't, they said they'd kill her.

"You do have a choice, Officer"—she flicked a look to his nametag—"Morell. This whole thing is falling apart. It has been for a while. You do realize that the reason they wanted Ben Deverall dead is because he has evidence that's going to bring this whole mess down, right?"

His lids flickered. "Be quiet."

"No." She shook her head. "Dev's got that evidence, and he's already given it to..." Her hesitation was brief and she hoped he didn't notice. She was making this shit up as she went and lying had never been one of her strong suits. She'd never thought she'd have reason to wish otherwise, until now. "The FBI. That's why that agent was there. That's why the BOLO was called off."

"Shut *up*," he said, voice going hard.

But she caught another clear thought.

I fucking knew it...

Movement behind him caught her attention and she fought not to betray anything. Joss.

"You didn't really think somebody was stupid enough to try to grab me in broad daylight, did you?" She threw the words out there. "Dev and Agent Crawford just made that shit up so they could have a valid reason for Crawford to go in and start feeling things out in the department."

Fuck, fuck, fuck!

That was all she caught from him that time.

She didn't understand why he was buying any of that bullshit, but she had to brazen it out.

A huge forearm snaked around Officer Morell's throat, joined by a weapon that pressed into the man's temple. The man went strangely still, not resisting at all.

"Take his weapon for me, will you, sweetheart?" Joss asked, his voice tight. "Do it fast."

She lurched up, not even questioning him. She remembered how he'd used his mind to grab Dev and had no doubt he was doing something similar to hold Officer Morell trapped, a prisoner in his own body.

She pried the gun from Morell's hand and fumbled with it until she was a few feet away, lowering it to her side with the muzzle pointed at the floor. She'd never held a gun in her life and the weight of it was monumental, pulling her entire arm to the ground, or so it seemed.

"What now?" she asked, voice trembling.

"This boy is going to take a few steps into the room or I'm going to ventilate his brain, that's what," Joss said, voice still tight, but a little less strained. "Come on, son. In you go."

In jerky, oddly reluctant movements—*Like a puppet's*, Nyrene thought—Morell moved into the room. Once inside, Joss said, "Nyrene, shut the door for me, would you?"

She scurried over and closed the door, then moved back across the room, still holding the gun.

"Stay where you're at now, sweetheart," Joss said, his drawl thicker, voice still tight. It hardened as he shifted his focus to the cop he still held in a vicious grip. "I'm going to let you go now, son. You're going to walk straight over to the chair and sit down. You do anything more than that, I'm going to do what you threatened to do to Nyrene—I'll shoot you in the knee, but not one knee, both of them. You won't even have to worry about riding a desk. Your days as a cop are *over.*"

He let Morell go and the big cop staggered a little.

Nyrene saw the struggle in his eyes, the internal battle being waged. And she saw the defeat that swam in his dark gaze. He accepted it and took one slow step, then another, toward the chair Joss had indicated. Halfway there, he stopped and turned around.

When he saw the gun Joss held pointed at knee level, he didn't even blink.

"If I give you names, will y'all make sure my wife gets protection?"

Joss inclined his head. "We would have done that anyway." Something that might have been a smile tipped up one corner of his mouth. "But you asking makes me think you might not be below the level of pond scum. You're just right on level with it."

Dev approached slowly, back to the wall of the house. The captain came in from the other side. Something vibrated in his pocket. His phone. He ignored it.

One step closer...another...another... The window was just a few steps away.

The vibrating started again just as he eased to the ground, ready to belly crawl under the window so he didn't cast a shadow through the curtains and betray his presence.

Hurry, hurry...

The vibrating stopped, but started again as soon as he regained his feet.

Then the door swung open and he dropped, weapon ready in a two-handed grip, aimed at chest level.

Joss stood there.

"Get your asses in here. We got this under control, but there's gonna to be a party. Don't want to ruin the surprise," the big man said in a cheery voice. He tossed a look behind him at the captain. "Good afternoon, Captain. It's been one hell of a day."

Then he ducked back into the house.

The adrenaline swirling in Dev had him ramped up so high, he was all but shaking with it as he stepped over the threshold of Nyrene's house, uncertain what he was going to find.

It wasn't anything he expected.

Officer Hank Morell sat in the same broken-in easy chair that Dev had used when he had come here that first night. Hell, had it even been a week? He had a grim set to his features and when he saw Dev, then the captain step through the door, his tanned features turned a dull shade of red.

Aww, fuck, Dev thought.

There was a quiet click of the door as the captain shut it.

"Morell. What brings you here?" Amana asked.

He shot her a look, then glanced at Dev. "You probably already know, Captain," the young cop said, voice emotionless.

Dev saw red.

Joss stepped in front of him. "I knew you were just a few minutes away so I made him go ahead and put in a call to the cop who brought him in on the mess. Let's not lose sight of the prize here."

As far as Dev was concerned, the *prize* was the dirty cop sitting in the middle of Nyrene's living.

Nyrene—

He turned his head, seeking her out.

She was curled up in the corner of her couch, clutching her purse to her chest in a familiar way. Her normally golden skin was pale and she gave him a wan smile. "He was going to shoot me in the knee," she said, her voice wobbling. "He told me we were going for a ride and I wouldn't go so he threatened to shoot me in the knee. I wouldn't go with him, though."

She delivered those words all without blinking an eye, and Dev was torn between rushing to her and turning on the cop who had put that look on her face.

"I ought to fucking kill you," he said in a low voice, not looking at Morell. If he did, his control would snap.

From the corner of his eye, he saw both the captain and Joss shift toward him. He laughed hollowly, shaking his head. "Eye on the prize, I know."

He retreated to a spot by the window, one that offered a clear view of the street while providing a decent level of obscurity for him. "Just when does this party get started?"

* * * * *

Larry Oman wasn't a happy man.

Not at all.

Morell had given him a terse call and told him there was a *problem* at the target's house and he needed Oman on site, ASAP. Then he'd hung up, refusing to answer Oman's two subsequent phone calls and then the single text he'd replied to had been as terse as the phone call.

Would you just get the fuck over here? There's a fucking mess.

Part of Oman was hoping the girl had gone and offed herself. Or maybe Dev had lost it and offed her. Or whoever had been feeding her intel, although none of those options were really the best, because he needed to know what the fuck she knew why Dev had been willing to risk his life to keep her with him and just what the general fuck was going on.

Without having those answers, he was in something of a mess himself.

And that was the *only* reason he was letting some dumbass, shit-for-brains uniform jerk him around.

Morell needed to watch himself.

Oman parked his car at the end of the driveway, effectively blocking the car in front of his. He took a quick look around the neighborhood, if one could call it that. There was a car down the street, parked on the side of the road. At the very far end, he caught sight of the front end of some sort of SUV on the cross street, but he couldn't make it out clearly. He did see the unmarked car that Morell drove, just a few doors down, and he had to shake his head. If that was where Morell had been watching her from, he'd probably been noticed.

Either by the girl or Deverall, although why in the hell either one of them was *here*, he didn't know. It was just another thing to worry about. As if he didn't have *enough*.

Grim, he mounted the steps as he cast one more look around the perimeter.

It was quiet, not even a bird calling to break the mid-afternoon silence. No cars driving down the street. Nothing.

Too quiet.

Uneasy, he reached down to try the door.

He found it unlocked and that didn't do shit to relieve his nerves.

Hinges creaked as the door swung open and he went for the weapon he carried in a holster secured under his left arm. As he nudged the door open wider, he drew his Glock and peered inside.

He caught sight of Morell's broad, muscled back in the middle of the room, standing there staring down at...something. Furniture blocked Oman's view and he couldn't see anything.

He didn't want to go inside, but it was too conspicuous to stand out here, so he slid in and shut the door, pressing his back to it after a quick look to make sure nobody waited there.

"Morell, what the fuck..."

Morell turned.

Oman swore at the sight of the man's hands, cuffed in front of him. There was also a piece of duct tape over his mouth, but judging by the look in Morell's eyes, neither the tape, nor the cuffs were necessary. Morell looked at Oman with seething hate, the same way he'd looked at him when Oman had threatened his wife if he fucked up the job.

"Guess me and your bitch are going to have some fun," Oman said without thinking.

A floorboard creaking had Oman looking away from Morell for the briefest moment. His gaze flicked back to Morell, but then slowly slid back to the doorway as Officer Bennett Deverall stepped through.

"I've got a better idea," Dev said. "How about you and me have some fun...bitch?"

CHAPTER SEVENTEEN

Oman immediately turned on him, his weapon jerking up. Dev didn't blink. He had no doubt that Oman would kill him if he had the chance, but Oman hadn't yet figured out that he was looking at three-on-one, and the odds weren't stacked in his favor.

Stepping deeper into the room, he kept Oman's attention on him, giving Joss a chance to come out of the bathroom down the hall.

He needed the cop to take just a step or two forward...

Oman took one.

It was a small step, but it should get him out of line of sight of the small bathroom just off the main room. If he could keep the man's attention on him.

Nyrene was tucked away in her bedroom on the far side of the house and as long no bullets started flying, she should be safe.

Safe.

He had less belief in that word now than ever before, but he was determined to do what he could to ensure her safety.

"Why did you kill Meredith, Oman?" he asked.

"I don't know what you're talking about," the other cop said, an easy smile on his face. "You really shouldn't have your gun drawn."

Dev didn't so much as blink. "You and me both know my weapon is holstered, Oman. You're the only one with a weapon out." Dev had intentionally left his weapon in the holster under his arm and he had no intention of drawing it unless he had to. Let Oman get cocky. Let him get stupid.

"You planning on killing me in cold blood?" Dev curled his lip at the other cop. "That ought to make the upcoming IAB investigation really interesting."

Oman's eyes flickered.

A floorboard creaked just as Joss appeared behind the dirty cop.

Oman went to spin around but Joss had already moved, putting the muzzle of his Glock snug against Oman's temple. "You don't want to be doing whatever it is you're thinking there," Joss said, his voice soft and easy. "If you do, I'll pull this trigger, and trust me, I'll have a much easier time explaining things to IAB than you will. After all, I'm not the one holding a gun on an unarmed man."

"Okay, I lied," Bennett said. "Maybe you're not the *only* one who is armed."

Oman had started to sweat.

It got even worse as Captain Amana revealed herself, stepping out of the kitchen, her own weapon in her hand and leveled at Oman. "Lower the weapon, Lieutenant," she said gently. "This is over."

"No." Oman sucked in a breath, then another, just shy of hyperventilating, it seemed.

What happened next happened so fast that Dev's mind went into overdrive just to handle it.

Oman shouted at him, the words a jumbled mess. Then he threw himself backward and sideways toward the door, away from the weapon Joss pointed at him. Dev didn't even remember drawing his own, but he found himself staring at Oman over the matte-black length of his Glock, his breathing slow, steady, heart slowing down as he prepared himself to pull the trigger.

But Oman was doing the same thing.

Only Oman had the muzzle of his gun pressed against the underside of his own chin.

"You think you're going to win this?" he said, panting.

"You dumb shit," Joss said.

Heavy tension filled the air in the next moment.

Face going purple, Oman started to lower his hand. But it was slow, like something was *forcing* the hand down.

"Son of a bitch," Dev muttered, recalling how something had grabbed him by the throat when he'd tried to get Joss to stop doing...whatever he'd been doing to Nyrene. It was the same tension in the air now that he'd felt then.

And, sure enough, when he looked at Oman's wrist, there were indentations, like a hand gripped him.

Those indentations pressed tighter and tighter as Oman's weapon hand was forced lower.

In a voice tense with strain, Joss said, "Do me a favor, Deverall. Relieve him of his weapon."

Amana, unaware of what was really happening, stirred next to him.

"What the *fuck* is happening?" Oman shouted.

Ignoring him, Dev took the weapon from a rigid hand. It was like prying something from the frozen grip of a corpse. Once he had it, he reversed the weapon in his hand and used it as a club, smacking Oman across the temple.

He dropped like a stone and Dev stood over him, breathing hard. "You don't get the easy way out, you chickenshit son of a bitch."

*   *   *   *   *

Amana was in the middle of arguing with Joss, insisting that Nyrene needed to come in and give a statement.

Dev didn't like the idea of her *not* being where he could watch over her, but he knew what Amana didn't— Nyrene had people looking out for her that regular cops just couldn't deal with.

He was trying to figure out how he was supposed to turn around and walk away from her now that his part in this fiasco was almost done.

He didn't know how he could.

Silently, he leaned against the counter in the kitchen while Nyrene sat at the table.

Four cop cars were parked out front. Morell was in one. Oman was in another.

An edgy tension filled Joss, something that Dev had picked up on the moment the cop cars had arrived. Nyrene was oddly quiet.

He didn't think he liked any of it.

He liked it even less when a knock sounded at the front door.

Nyrene tensed, looking up from her cup of tea with an

odd, almost mechanical movement. She got up and he watched as she made her way into the small living room, one made even smaller by the dynamic presences of Amana and Joss Crawford.

Nyrene stood there in the doorway and smoothed her hands down her pants.

"It's Taige," she said, the words coming out dull and listless.

"About fucking time," Joss muttered. He gestured to the door.

Nyrene shifted from foot to foot, her reluctance so obvious Dev wanted to tell all of them to get the hell out of her house.

But he didn't.

Instead, he edged around her and paused at her side, brushing his fingers down her arm. "Why don't you sit? I'll get it."

Night was coming on now and while he didn't know what it was that had tension vibrating inside her, he suspected it had to do with the woman on the other side of the door. He knew Taige wanted Nyrene to help them lure in some of the people from this so-called Psychic Portal, but he thought she'd already done enough.

As he opened the door, he searched for the right phrase to make the woman standing on the porch see that.

But he took one look at her and realized it was a waste of time.

She met his eyes levelly, the gray hard and uncompromising. To his surprise, she didn't force her way inside. "She has done enough, but they don't care."

Delivered as simply as that, and he knew.

"They're coming, aren't they?" he asked.

Taige inclined her chin.

"Fuck." Stepping aside, he let Taige enter.

He could tell the captain recognized Taige Morgan by the way Amana's jaw dropped, her normal unflappable attitude completely...well, *flapped*. Amana's blue eyes blinked rapidly as she locked on Taige's face and she reached up to smooth her hair back before, finally, she took a step forward, one hand outstretched.

"You're Taige Morgan."

Taige glanced at her, then accepted the offered hand. "I am. Captain, I hate to be blunt, but I need you and your cops to get the hell out of here."

Amana blinked at the terse delivery.

Then she skimmed her eyes around the room, let her gaze linger on Joss before she slanted it back to Taige. After a moment, she nodded. But before she turned for the door, she looked at Deverall. "I expect some sort of explanation."

"I don't know how much I can tell you."

"Just..." She waved a hand. "Tell me something."

CHAPTER EIGHTEEN

After everything that had happened, it all ended with very little fanfare.

Nyrene had expected...*something*. Some sort of climactic build-up.

Dev had left to go with his captain, and that had been with a lot more fanfare than with what later happened. He'd only left because Taige bluntly said, "We can hide the fact that we're here. But you *can't*. Your presence, even *now,* could be fucking things up. You want her safe or not?"

So he'd left, not even saying a word to Nyrene and damn if *that* didn't hurt.

Joss and Taige were in the kitchen, leaning up against the counter and talking quietly.

Nyrene was in her room, pretending to pack.

She had no idea where she was supposed to be going, but it wasn't like she was going to sit around waiting for people to come and grab her. Taige had told her to act natural, do what she'd have done under normal circumstances. She'd told Taige that under normal circumstances, she'd have been packing up and hauling ass.

So Taige told her to do it.

It wasn't hard to feign what was almost panicked motions as she went through her wardrobe and took out what was the most important, putting it in a suitcase. She'd been at it for almost an hour.

When she had the suitcase full and nobody showed up, she'd go to Taige, give her a look and Taige would just shake her head. So she'd start all over again.

She had no idea how long this was supposed to take

and although she *was* feeling panicky, it was hard to maintain that level of energy for too long.

She was about ready to crash.

Or so she thought.

Something rolled across her senses. She had no idea what it was. The only way she could describe it was like a *knock*—somebody tap, tap, tapping against the window of her soul, just checking to see if she was there.

Panic, *true* panic exploded inside her and she rushed to the door, mouth open.

Joss was already there and he lifted a hand, covered her mouth.

He shook his head in warning and then nodded back to the bedroom. She gave him a pained look. If she was supposed to be doing what her instincts said, then she should be hauling ass—like *now*.

But Joss shook his head and gave her another hard glare.

She withdrew, her gaze flicking to meet Taige's.

Taige gave her a reassuring smile and held up a note. The writing on it was a scrawl and Nyrene had the impression it had been written quickly.

Take a suitcase. Go into the living room. Act like you're leaving. Wait until the time is right. You'll know.

Taige had a lot more confidence in her than Nyrene had in herself, but she nodded, feeling defeated.

The suitcase was about as full as it needed to be, so she zipped it shut.

That odd tension had settled into a vibration of sorts at the base of her skull. It all but hummed. *Be ready, be ready, be ready...*

Nyrene hefted the suitcase off the bed, watched as Taige slipped into her room to take her place, turning off the light and closing the door until only a couple of inches remained open.

Joss hit the lights in the kitchen and remained in there, lurking in the shadows.

Nyrene turned to look at him, mouth opening to ask him a question.

But it froze on her lips as a trail of ice seemed to trip up her spine.

Slowly, she turned toward the door.

You'll know.

Her breathing hitched in her lungs.

She wanted to *run*.

Everything inside her *screamed* it.

Although her instincts, now in full-on panic mode, chittered at her and insisted there might not be any time left *to* run. *He'll hurt you,* they whispered. *They told him he could hurt you if you didn't come. He likes hurting people.*

She had no idea who *he* was.

Then a fist hit the door.

"Nyrene?"

A man's voice called out her name.

She couldn't speak.

He knocked again, louder this time. "Open up, Nyrene. I can feel you in there."

Feel me? Panic screamed louder.

Joss's voice drifted to her. *"Say something,"* he whispered, almost soundlessly. "It's okay. You're not alone."

She sure as hell felt like it.

Gripping the handle of her suitcase, she said in a wavering voice, "Who is it?"

"A friend, Nyrene. I'm a friend. I'm here to help with this problem of yours."

She wanted to scream out she didn't have a problem, that her only problem was all the people who wouldn't quit following her, but she said nothing.

She didn't know what *to* say. There was nothing that wouldn't sound like a bald-faced lie.

Swallowing the knot in her throat, she backed away from the door instinctively. She had barely lifted her foot when the doorknob rattled a little.

"Oh, honey," the man said on the other side of the door. "Locks are useless with me."

Her fingers tightened until the plastic grip of the suitcase handle was biting into her skin. She made it two more steps as she watched, mesmerized, while the lock slowly twisted in the other direction, going from the *locked* position to the *unlocked*. Heart pounding, she backed up one more step as the doorknob turned and the door started to squeak open.

A couple of low murmurs were exchanged and she realized for the first time that he wasn't alone.

She swallowed back the whimper rising in her throat and tottered back a couple more steps.

She tried to tell herself that Joss and Taige were there with her and they seemed confident that they could handle these people, that they knew what they were doing. She was fine, she *had* to be fine.

But none of the mental pep talking she tried to offer did anything to soothe the ragged, jarring fear unfurling inside her gut.

The door opened completely and a man appeared in the doorway. With him was a woman, her head almost on level with his, and the man wasn't exactly short.

Her pale hair caught the lights from the streets and the few dim ones Nyrene had on in the living room. Liquid-blue eyes skimmed the room, coming to rest on Nyrene and a small smile curved her lips before she glanced past her into the dark kitchen just beyond Nyrene's shoulders. Standing behind the man, he didn't see the way she lifted a finger to her lips.

Shhh...it's a secret, she seemed to say to Nyrene.

What? Nyrene wanted to scream. *What's a secret?*

The man stepped forward, speaking. "Nyrene?"

She cleared her throat and backed up another step, almost to the kitchen now. "Who are you? What are you doing in my house?"

"I'm here to help," he said easily. "Phantom told you I'd be coming. Remember?"

She tensed at the sound of that name. Phantom.

Jerking her eyes to the woman, she waited, wondering if this was the mysterious Phantom.

But the woman just smiled. "I'm just along for the ride, honey. It's all good."

The man's face folded into a frown and he glanced back at the woman. It was...odd. Nyrene couldn't think of any other way to describe it. It was almost as if he'd forgotten she was there. But the woman reached out and caught his wrist, squeezing lightly. "Don't you have something to do?"

A faint line appeared between her brows as she spoke, but when she pulled her hand away, the man muttered, "I've got a job. Stupid fucking bitches...always hauling stupid fucking bitches around."

His gaze locked on Nyrene and the air dwindled out of her lungs.

"We're going to take a ride."

"No," Nyrene said, squaring her shoulders.

He smiled. "I was hoping you'd say that."

Her blood ran cold.

But as he took a step toward her, the lights in the kitchen flared on.

Joss moved to join her.

The man tensed.

"Who the fuck are you?" he demanded, the hand at his side clenching into a tight fist.

"Somebody who isn't too keen on letting Nyrene go for a ride," Joss replied easily. He glanced at the blonde standing silently behind the unbelievably plain man— plainly dressed, plain-looking. Everything about him was *plain.* "Lousy company you keep these days, Nalini."

Nyrene jerked at that.

The woman slid Joss a sly grin. "I was in the middle of getting information out of him when he got a call. I wasn't done. Figured I'd just come along for the ride."

The man, once more, shot Nalini a confused look. She repeated what she'd done earlier, taking his wrist and squeezing.

His face folded back into the irritated lines it had been in when he'd seen Joss.

"You need to just step out of the way, big guy, if you don't want to get hurt," the man said, directing a sneer at Joss.

"Nah." Joss smiled, then tossed a look over his shoulder. "You know, I was really wanting to play with you myself, but that comment about stupid fucking bitches changed my mind. Hey, honey, why don't you come on out?"

Nyrene refused to keep shrinking away. So far, the man hadn't so much as moved for her and Joss stood next to her—big, muscled, ready.

And somehow, she realized the woman wasn't there to harm her, either.

Then footsteps sounded on the floor. *Click, click, click* went the heels of Taige's boots.

The man's eyes flicked to Taige, then fell away, before

shooting right back to her.

It was...comical.

His gaze went wide and his jaw fell open.

He backed away from the woman who'd just entered the room and Taige smiled.

It was a cat's smile, and when he kept backing up, she just laughed.

He smacked straight into the blonde who ended up spinning him around and grabbing his face in her hands. "Let's just end this little game now, shall we?"

CHAPTER NINETEEN

"You can live here, if you want."

Nyrene looked at the small cottage and fought the urge to laugh with not a little hysteria.

Her entire life had been upended.

She had gone from being a boring nurse who longed to be a romance writer to a psychic who longed to be a boring nurse, and Taige had just offered her a chance to be a nurse again.

I need somebody with your skills. It's not like I can put an ad in the paper. Not everybody knows this shit exists, Nyrene. We need to keep it that way.

She was going to have a chance to live rent free and Taige had also mentioned sending her back to school for her RN and paying for accelerated courses in trauma—and business management.

When Nyrene asked why, Taige had grimaced. *I need somebody who can help with administration shit. You seem like a good fit.*

But Nyrene didn't need classes in that. She'd been helping run Dr. Evil's office for almost two years, ever since he'd chased off the last office manager. She and Michelle had been doing the job together, so it was entirely likely she could fumble her way through whatever it was that Taige needed.

"Will you tell me more about what happened that day?" she asked, turning to look at the woman who'd be her boss. "Will you teach me to control...this?"

She waved a hand at her head.

"You were there," Taige said softly. "What do you

think happened? And I already promised to help teach you. That's already a given."

"I don't know what happened with that woman. Who she is. Why she was there."

"I can't tell you much about her, but she's...trustworthy," Taige said, leaning her hips against the bed. Her brow arched up and she coolly said, "You're not law enforcement material, Nyrene. You're not a cop. You're not...one of us. But that doesn't mean you can't use this gift of yours to help people. I can show you how. I'm offering you that chance."

Nyrene knew that.

She also knew that her old life was gone.

There was no way to go back to it, either.

Still, she thought about Dev, thought about the hint of a promise she'd thought was maybe growing between them.

"I'm a danger out there right now, aren't I?" she whispered.

"You could be," Taige allowed. "I won't stop you from living your life, but it's possible you could bring harm to those around you, especially if you slip and your shields fall."

Her decision was already made.

The fact that Taige had just told her she wouldn't be forced was just one more brick in the wall.

"I want to be able to make a difference," she said, her voice hollow.

"Honey..." Taige came up and rested a hand on her shoulder. "You already have."

* * * * *

Dev came up short at the sight of the woman leaning against the back of the rental. His personal vehicle had been impounded and Amana was already taking care of getting it turned back over to him, but for now, he'd need the rental for at least one more night.

He hoped Crawford had worked things out on that end before he'd up and disappeared a couple of hours ago.

And shit, had he disappeared.

Dev had gotten a text from him around six, letting

him know that everything had gone down smoothly and Taige had Nyrene tucked away for the night. Crawford, according to the text, had to report back to his own boss, but it had been mighty nice working with him.

Dev had been in the middle of talking to the captain so he hadn't been able to answer right away. It took him all of ten minutes to get some room to answer and in those ten minutes, the number Joss had texted him from had been disconnected.

What the fuck had he meant, Taige had Nyrene tucked away for the night?

Where the hell *was* Nyrene?

The first thing he planned to do when he left the station was to go to Nyrene's house, although he knew he wouldn't find her there. And his plans didn't change even when he was kept at the Clary Police Department until nearly midnight.

He was going to track down Nyrene, come hell or high water.

The sight of the long, lean woman standing with one hip propped against his car sort of changed the equation though. Having Taige standing less than ten feet away meant he might not have to track down Nyrene.

"Where the hell is Nyrene?" he demanded, closing the distance between himself and the quiet psychic with strange gray eyes.

Taige lifted a brow. "Hello, Deverall. Good to see you. How did everything go down? Man, it's been a crazy few days, huh?" She spoke in a laconic drawl laced with humor.

He had no time for it. "Where is she?"

"She's at my facility," Taige said calmly. "She wants to learn. I can't teach her anywhere else, and she needs hands-on training. This isn't the kind of thing that comes with an online course and a syllabus." Taige hitched up one shoulder in a shrug. "Besides, while we eliminated the one group that was trailing after her, there's no guarantee more won't come looking. Once she's fully trained, she'll be safer, but we need to track down the people who put the alert on her for her to be *really* safe."

"You're..." Ben narrowed his eyes. "It almost sounds like she's there under watch."

"No." Taige smiled serenely. "We're a private facility. She's not being detained or anything else. She wants to be there." She shoved off his car and moved to stand in front of him. "Of course, if you don't trust me, you're welcome to come and talk to her for yourself."

In response, Dev pulled out his keys. "I'll follow you."

She made a face. "Well, about that... I think it will work better if you ride with me. See, my car is clean and I really don't feel like crawling around on the ground checking yours for bugs."

He wanted to argue but logic sort of insisted she had a point.

Plus, the longer he argued, the longer it would take to see Nyrene.

And wasn't it just a bitch that suddenly he was the one who was going to be just along for the ride?

Maybe it was karma paying him a visit.

"Fine," he said, moving to the car parked next to his. "I'm assuming this is yours."

"Man, you must be psychic," she said lightly.

* * * * *

He'd planned to be awake at first light and hunt down Nyrene. By the time they'd gotten to Taige's mysterious *facility*, it had been past four a.m.

He'd assumed he'd have to go to a hotel, but Taige had told him there were a few guest rooms in the facility and she'd put him up for the night.

His head had no sooner hit the pillow than he was out.

It was the first deep sleep he'd had in months.

When the bright light shining in through the window finally managed to wake him, he jackknifed into an upright position, looking around, disoriented.

His limbs weighed down on him like his muscles had turned to concrete overnight but he knew the real culprit was his own exhaustion. He'd been running on fumes and adrenaline for so long, and at some point last night his gut had decided he was safe, so instinct had shut down and the adrenaline fueling him had just crashed.

He felt like shit.

Fumbling his way out of the bed, he half-walked, half-stumbled into the bathroom he remembered passing on his way to the bed last night.

Once he'd taken care of urgent matters, he splashed water on his face, then made judicious use of the wrapped toothbrush.

He wasn't feeling much more human even after he'd taken care of basic hygiene needs.

But he wasn't waiting around to see Nyrene, either.

Scrubbing his hands over his face, he made his way to the door and opened it.

Immediately, he came up short.

There was a slim teenage boy waiting there.

He caught sight of Dev and flashed him a smile. "Hello, I'm Alex," the boy said, the faintest hint of an accent underscoring the words. "Ms. Morgan wanted me to wait for you and bring you to her."

"I—" He started to say *I don't want to see Taige*, but decided it wasn't ideal to have that discussion with a kid. He'd just have it with Taige instead. Falling into step with the boy, he studied his surroundings. He hadn't known what to expect from Taige's facility, but it seemed an awful lot like a *home*. "Do you...um..."

"This is my home. Sort of," Alex said cheerfully.

"What's that mean—sort of?"

"I'm being trained." The boy shrugged, as if he was discussing the weather. "My uncle and his wife are with the Bureau, but that's not really any place I can get training. Ms. Morgan, though? She's good at helping with that. Especially after..." His words trailed to an end and he said, "We're here."

Dev wanted to ask, *After what?*

But Alex had already opened the door to the room.

Music flowed out. It was that new-age sort of stuff—instrumental, all harps and fluid, liquid sounds that went perfectly with the people on the floor in front of him. As he watched, they went from standing with their arms overhead to dropping down with their hands brushing the floor.

His eyes locked in on one curvy ass.

How pathetic was it that he knew from one look that he was staring at Nyrene's excellent butt?

He didn't know.

The boy next to him cleared his throat.

Dev shot a look at him and saw that the boy's golden cheeks were flushed a ruddy shade and he was making a study of the very plain ceiling overhead.

"Shit, kid," Dev said. "If you don't want to know what I'm thinking, try harder not to hear it. *I* can't help it."

"So I noticed," the boy responded with a snicker.

The sound of their voices carried and somebody from the front called for a break.

Nyrene straightened and turned around, face flushed pink as her gaze collided with his.

"Ben," she murmured.

And even though it seemed like twenty feet separated them, he heard that murmur as though she'd whispered it right into his ear.

CHAPTER TWENTY

On their way out the door, Taige pushed a closed envelope into his hand. "Read it. Oh, hell, I don't know. You'll figure it out. You're looking for something. Maybe it's an answer," she said.

Then she called the class together, minus Nyrene.

She'd informed Nyrene she'd given her a little slack as she was still trying to settle in, but within a week, Nyrene's slack would be *gone.*

Nyrene glanced over her shoulder as the door shut, then met his eyes. "If she calls this slack, I don't want to know how it gets when it's slackless," she said gamely.

Her skin was still flushed, and when they reached a water fountain up in front of them, she paused and refilled her water bottle. She emptied half of it standing there and refilled it.

"Yoga making you thirsty?" he asked.

"It's not just the *yoga,*" she said, a pained look on her face. "It's...everything. I had to get up and go *running* this morning. I was up at seven a.m. to go running. I've never run a day in my life. But Taige was hounding me about how all of this"—she waved a hand at her head—"takes discipline, and if I can discipline my body, then having discipline over my brain will be a lot easier. Thus the running and the *yoga.* Although she said the yoga is both mental and physical discipline."

They pushed through the doors on the right and Nyrene sighed. "There are chairs out here. That kid Alex mentioned them earlier."

"You seem at home already," Dev said, starting to

wonder if he even needed to be there.

"I..." She stopped and shook her head. "I can't say I feel at home. But I can breathe." A faint smile curled her lips as she turned to look at him. "I don't have a hundred thoughts weighing in on me so even though I'm maintaining my shields, nothing weighs them down. It's like the difference between holding an umbrella over your head on a nice day when there's no rain and a stormy day with hail and wind."

"But it's the stormy days when you need the umbrella," he pointed out.

"I know." Her full lips turned down in a grimace as she added, "But I never learned how to really do any of this. I don't have the...muscle for it. So it's all that much more exhausting."

"Then you're fine with being here."

"I *need* to be here," she said simply. "Not just to learn, but because..." She hesitated, licking her lips as she struggled to find the words. "It's going to take me some time to learn what I need to learn, Ben. And I don't want to be a burden while I'm doing it. Here, I don't have to be. Taige needs a nurse on hand. She runs a school here for the younger psychics they come across. There's also a business—security stuff, but she has other people who help head that up. Sometimes people get hurt and unless it's super serious, they avoid hospitals. It's just too complicated coming up with explanations for things like..." She shot him a nervous smile. "How would we explain it if one of us had gotten hurt the past few days? People would think we were crazy."

"It's not just training you want then?" The words tasted bitter in his throat. He felt like he was at loose ends now. He didn't really want to go back to the Clary Police Department, but it was all he knew. He didn't want to leave Clary because that was where she was, or he'd thought it was where she'd be.

"I'm trying to make a life for myself," she said softly. "I've never had one."

He turned away. "That's...well, good for you, Nyrene." He had to clear his throat to force out the words. "I'm happy for you."

He tried to will his legs to move—one step. That was all he needed to do, take one step.

But he couldn't do it.

"They said there was a reason," Nyrene said behind him.

He looked back over his shoulder at her.

She edged closer, looking beautiful in skin-hugging pants and a close-fitting top. Her hair was swept up into a ponytail and her eyes looked incredibly dark, incredibly beautiful.

"I think part of the reason was because I was meant to save you," she said. "I think that's part of the reason all of this happened."

"Yeah." He nodded slowly. "I think so, too."

She took another step and he turned to face her, although logically he needed to get the hell out of there. Leave, before he started to beg.

"But I think there's another reason you and I ended up running across each other's path, Bennett Deverall," she said softly. "I think we were meant to."

She reached up and touched his cheek.

His heart slammed against his ribs as he covered her hand with his own. "Nyrene?"

She leaned in closer, letting him take some of her weight.

"Don't you feel...something here?" She bit her lip after asking, indecision on her face, but then, after taking a breath, she pushed on. "I mean, I know we just met, and everything's been crazy, but I felt something for you practically from the second I met you, even when I was crying all over you."

"You...this..." He fisted his hand, only to have paper crumple in his fist.

Confused, he looked down and saw the envelope Taige had given him.

Nyrene continued to talk.

"I know you've got a job in Clary and I'm here, but maybe we can work something out."

You're looking for something. Maybe it's an answer, Taige had said. He'd been looking for something for a while. But how could Taige have any clue?

Dumbass, that voice inside him whispered. *She's psychic.*

He turned away from Nyrene and opened the envelope.

Inside it, he found two pieces of paper.

The first one... He blinked and shook his head, immediately flipping to the next.

Then he just stared.

After a few seconds, he started to laugh.

Nyrene harrumphed behind him. "You know, I don't really see what's—"

He turned to her, crossing the paved stones to catch the back of her neck in one hand, hauling her up against him for a kiss. He swallowed down the rest of her comment, wishing he could just eat her up in five or six greedy bites, but this wasn't the time or place.

"I won't be in Clary," he said, breaking the kiss.

She blinked up at him.

"You won't?"

"No." He pulled her up against him, smiling down at her, feeling lighter than he had in...*months*. "Taige just offered me a job."

Deverall,

Like I said, you're looking for something. So am I. I need a cop. Most of my people are young and even some of the people who aren't come to me without any law enforcement training. What we do, we do by instinct. But instinct doesn't trump real training.

What do you think about coming on board here and working with my people?

I don't just mean being a teacher, either. There are cases we get that need the brains of a cop on them. I want you to be that cop.

Let me know what you think.

It was signed simply,

Taige

Did you enjoy this title?
Sign up for Shiloh's newsletter to stay up to date on all her new releases.
www.shilohwalker.com/website/

THIS STORY WAS READER-FUNDED.

Without the support of my Patreon readers, this book wouldn't have become a reality.

My Patreon reader base has already funded three works, including this title, Haunted Blade and Damon, a short story that was a patron-exclusive but can now be read in the special anniversary collection of Blade Song.

Want to join these patrons and help in future projects? These include additional FBI Psychics story, the next Kit Colbana story and more.

Visit my Patreon site at

www.patreon.com/Shilohwalker for more info. Pledge levels start at $1.00 and rewards are offered at every level.

READ THE MISSING

Book 1 in the FBI Psychics Series

After all these years...she'd known she'd see him again. Even when she drove away from Cullen Morgan's home in tears, she'd known it wasn't over between them.

Why he was coming to her now, she didn't know and honestly, just then, she didn't care.

She was so desperate to see him again, it was almost pathetic.

No, it was pathetic. It had been twelve years, and she was all but panting at the thought of seeing him, of staring into those amazing eyes and standing close enough to smell him. How much had he changed? Taige wondered. Instinctively, she knew that Cullen would be as devastating at thirty-three as he'd been at twenty-one. The truck came to a stop close to the house. She couldn't see anything beyond the back bumper, and when the taillights went off, she jerked as though somebody had used a Taser on her.

She took a deep breath and then groaned as her shirt dragged against her nipples. They were stiff and erect, throbbing under the thin layer of cotton. Embarrassed, she folded her arms over them and wished she could manage to get a damn bra on. Her hand hurt too much to manage it, though.

Facing Cullen braless and in her bare feet: how much more disconcerting could it get? She held herself stiff as the knock came, pounding on the door as though he wanted to tear the door from its hinges. It came a second time, and third. Finally, she made herself move, shuffling through the dark living room with her arms crossed over her breasts, the wrap on her cast abrading the bare skin of her left arm and rubbing against her nipples.

Nerves jangled in her belly. No butterflies; this felt more like she had giant gryphons taking flight inside her, gryphons with knife-edged wings. She reached out and closed her left hand around the doorknob and slowly opened it, half hiding behind the door. She kept her gaze focused straight ahead so that all she saw was the way his white T-shirt stretched across his wide, muscled chest.

Through her peripheral vision, she saw that he held something in his hand. Something clutched so tight, his knuckles had gone white. She hissed out a breath and forced herself to look upward, up, up, up until she was staring into his eyes. It took a little longer than it should have; he was taller than he had been. At least by an inch. She was five foot ten—she didn't have to look up to many people, and she decided then that she didn't care for it at all.

"Taige."

She didn't say anything. She couldn't. Her throat felt frozen, and forcing words past her frozen vocal chords seemed impossible. She just stepped aside to let him come in, and when he did, his arm brushed against hers. She flinched and pulled away, backing away until a good two feet separated them. Once he was inside, she closed the door and leaned against it, resting her left hand on the doorknob and holding her right hand against her belly and studying the floor.

He turned to stare at her. From under her lashes, she watched as his shoulders rose and fell, his chest moving as he blew out a harsh breath, almost like he'd been holding his breath the same way she had.

"God, Taige..."

His voice sounded almost exactly like it had in her dreams—no, exactly. In the dim light, she couldn't see his face very well, but she had a bad, bad feeling that her dreams had been pretty damn accurate in that aspect, too. Shoving away from the door, she kept her head down as she moved around him and headed into the living room. He followed behind her slowly. She heard a click, and light flooded the room. She shot him a look over her shoulder, just a quick glance, enough to tell her just how dead-on her dreams had been.

It was almost too spooky; even his hair looked right. It was shorter than it had been when he was younger, almost brutally short. His shoulders strained the seams of his shirt, and she had a flashback to her last dream, when he had crowded her up against the couch, demanding she tell him how she'd gotten hurt. She'd shoved him, pushing one hand against one wide, rock-hard shoulder, and she imagined if she reached out and touched him, he'd feel exactly like he had in her dreams.

"So, are you going to look at me or just let me stare at the back of your head all night?" he asked softly.

She shot him another quick, almost nervous glance over her shoulder, and Cullen blew out a breath.

When he spoke again, his voice was closer. "Aren't you going to ask me why I'm here?"

Aren't you going to speak to me at all? Cullen wanted to ask.

Instead, he waited until she finally turned around and faced him. In the brightly lit room, he noticed two things. The first was that she had her arm, her right arm, in a cast that went halfway up to her elbow. A chill raced down his spine. The second was that her left eye was puffy and nearly swollen shut, a dark, ugly bruise that Cullen suspected was every bit as painful as it looked.

"I already know why you're here. You need my help." A bitter smile curved her lips as she stared at him. "Why would else would you be here?" She glanced at the file in his hand and held out her hand.

Cullen swallowed and lifted it, staring at it with the metallic taste of fear thick in his mouth. "You don't owe me a damn thing, Taige. I know that. I've got no right being here, and I know that, too."

She sighed and dropped her head, covering her eyes with her uninjured hand. "Cullen, stop. You want something. Out with it. I've got better things to do than stand here and have you brooding all over me. So just spill it."

"I...look, if I didn't have to have your help, I wouldn't be here. But it's not me that needs you—just...just don't—"

Taige cocked a brow. "You don't have much of an opinion of me, do you, Cullen? Whatever brought you here in the middle of the night twelve years after kicking me out of your life has to be pretty damn important, and considering the kind of help you probably need, I'm going to assume there's somebody else involved." She stared at him, her gaze shuttered. "You think so little of me that I'd refuse to help whoever this is just to make you suffer because you and me got some history?"

History... Is that what we had?

Read more at shilohwalker.com

BIO

Shiloh Walker has been writing since she was a kid. She fell in love with vampires with the book Bunnicula and has worked her way up to the more...ah...serious works of fiction. Once upon a time she worked as a nurse, but now she writes full time and lives with her family in the Midwest. She writes romantic suspense and contemporary romance, and urban fantasy under her penname, J.C. Daniels (http://jcdanielsblog.com/).

Join the Newsletter
Monthly contests are held.
You can win free books!

Join Shiloh Online

BB bookbub.com/authors/shiloh-walker

 @twitter.com/shilohwalker

www.facebook.com/AuthorShilohWalker

CHECK SHILOH'S OTHER HALF...J.C. DANIELS

J.C. Daniels' Titles
Blade Song #1
Night Blade #2
Broken Blade #3
Edged Blade #4
Shadowed Blade #5
A Stroke of Dumb Luck (Tor)
Bladed Magic (A Kit Colbana Novella)
Misery's Way (A Kit Colbana Novella)
Final Protocol
Blade Song Anniversary Edition
Damon

LOOK FOR OTHER TITLES BY SHILOH WALKER

The Grimm
Urban Fantasy Romance
Candy Houses • No Prince Charming • Crazed
Hearts

The Ash Trilogy
If You Hear Her • If You See Her • If You Know
Her

The Secrets & Shadows Series
Burn For Me • Break For Me • Long For Me
Deeper Than Need • Sweeter Than Sin • Darker
Than Desire

The FBI Psychics
The Missing • The Departed • The Reunited
The Protected • The Unwanted • The Innocent

The Hunters
Paranormal Romance
Hunting the Hunter • Hunters: Heart and Soul •
Hunter's Salvation
Hunter's Need • Hunter's Fall • Hunter's Rise

Printed in Great Britain
by Amazon